"Who are you, anyway? I don't even know your name."

"Lazaro Herrera."

The name rolled off his tongue: fluid, complex, sensual. The rs trilled, the z was accented, the vowels so rich and smoky they could have been aged whiskey.

Lazaro Herrera.

It was a name that fit him, a name that echoed strength and muscle and power.

"I think I'll take that drink," she whispered.

His fingers brushed hers as he handed her the glass. "Sip it. Slowly."

His skin was warm, yet his touch scalded her. She nearly dropped the glass.

"Why are you doing this?"

He shrugged, a vague shift of his massive shoulders.

"I have reasons."

"But what did I d

"This isn't about

"Then what is it

"Revenge."

Jane Porter was born in California, USA, and spent her teens and early twenties living abroad. During her time in the UK Jane discovered Mills and Boon®, and read the books under the bedcovers so her mother wouldn't find out. Now a teacher, with an MA in Writing, Jane lives in Seattle with her husband and two small boys. She says she plots books in between teaching her eldest son to read and changing her baby's nappies!

LAZARO'S REVENGE is Jane's fifth book in the Modern Romance™ series.

Recent titles by the same author:

THE ITALIAN GROOM
CHRISTOS'S PROMISE
THE SHEIKH'S WIFE
IN DANTE'S DEBT

LAZARO'S REVENGE

BY
JANE PORTER

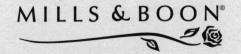

All the characters in this book have no existence outside the imagination of the author, and have no relation whatsoever to anyone bearing the same name or names. They are not even distantly inspired by any individual known or unknown to the author, and all the incidents are pure invention.

First published in Great Britain 2002
Harlequin Mills & Boon Limited,
Eton House, 18-24 Paradise Road, Richmond, Surrey TW9 1SR

© Jane Porter-Gaskins 2002

ISBN 0 263 82931 6

Set in Times Roman 10½ on 12½ pt.
01-0502-40579

Printed and bound in Spain
by Litografia Rosés, S.A., Barcelona

PROLOGUE

"I DON'T kidnap women," Lazaro Herrera retorted grimly, his back to the plate-glass window overlooking Buenos Aires's fashionable Avenida Sante Fe boulevard. "I might have a reputation for being ruthless, but that's business, not personal."

"Sometimes I'm not sure if it *isn't* personal," Dante Galván answered, almost as an aside.

Lazaro turned sharply to face the man who headed Galván Enterprises, and the only man Lazaro answered to. Dante might be chief executive officer but as president, Lazaro was the acting manager. "Even I have scruples, and I draw the line at kidnapping."

"You're misinterpreting me. I never said *kidnap*. Zoe is my wife's younger sister. She's just twenty-two. All I want to do is to protect her."

Lazaro's gaze narrowed speculatively. "Protect Daisy, you mean." Dante didn't say anything and Lazaro's mouth twisted grimly. "Neither you nor Daisy like this American, Carter Scott—"

"For good reasons, mind you."

"So what you're really doing is shielding Daisy from unpleasant news."

Dante didn't immediately answer. His mouth pressed tight, his features pinched. Dark purple shadows formed crescents beneath his amber eyes. "Daisy can't lose this baby. She can't handle this right now,

5

can't handle more bad news, and I'll be damned if I let her suffer through another miscarriage.''

Pain throbbed in Dante's voice, pain and anger and helplessness. Lazaro knew about Daisy's two previous miscarriages. The second one occurred last year, and fairly late in the pregnancy. Daisy had been devastated by the loss and Dante had taken six weeks off from work to be with Daisy as she convalesced at the *estancia*. It was then Lazaro had completely taken over management of the corporation.

Unfortunately, Dante didn't know he was playing straight into Lazaro's hands. Dante didn't know that every move he made, every bit of power he relinquished, only strengthened Lazaro's position, and weakened his own.

''I'm lucky to have you,'' Dante said quietly. ''If it weren't for you, we'd all be in trouble.''

Lazaro tensed, his conscience pricked by Dante's earnest gratitude. He hated the tug of contradictory emotions within him and turned to face the window where Buenos Aires's skyline sparkled in the sunshine.

For the first time in a long time, he despised what he'd started here, with the Galváns.

He despised the secrets he kept buried in his heart, despised the thing that drove him to destroy Dante and the Galváns, but it was too late to change the course now.

Yet even as he stood at the window, weighted by memories of a dark past, he felt Dante's worry for Daisy, felt Dante's own burden, and longed to warn

Dante to be careful. *Don't trust me. Don't feel safe with me. Don't let me close to your family.*

But Lazaro didn't speak. He stifled the guilt and sense of obligation, telling himself that Dante's problems weren't his problems. Dante's pain wasn't his pain. Dante's loss wasn't his loss.

Lazaro drew a deep breath, hardened his emotions, and reminded himself that this wasn't a simple feud. It was revenge. More than revenge.

It was about one's soul.

His mother's.

Ice sheeting his heart, Lazaro turned from the city glittering with sunshine to face his secret arch rival. ''What's the plan?''

CHAPTER ONE

"BE quiet, do as you're told, and everything will be fine."

She'd been kidnapped—abducted in the middle of the day from Ezeiza International Airport in Buenos Aires in full view of airport security.

Zoe Collingsworth's stomach plummeted as the helicopter tilted sideways and flew at a peculiar angle to the earth below.

She gripped her boxy seat tighter, fingers clenched so hard that the knuckles ached. He'd told her not to talk and she hadn't, but she was very afraid. This couldn't really be happening…this had to be a bad dream…

"We'll be landing in a few minutes."

She jerked at the sound of his voice. It was the first time he'd spoken in the two hours they'd been aboard the helicopter. She'd never heard a voice pitched so low and it rumbled through her like a slow-moving freight train.

"Where are you taking me?" she whispered, hands trembling.

He briefly glanced her way, his narrowed eyes barely resting on her. "It doesn't matter."

Her mouth went dry, fear sucking heat from her limbs. She touched her seat belt, checking the tension in the belt, as though the small firm strap across her lap could somehow protect her from whatever was to come next.

She wanted to say something fierce and defiant, wanted to be brave because that's how Daisy handled problems. But Zoe wasn't a warrior woman and she felt the worst kind of terror imaginable. She'd never even been out of Kentucky before, and now on her first trip anywhere she was…she was…

Kidnapped.

Her heart thudded so fast and hard she thought it might explode. She stared at her captor. He wasn't looking at her, but staring out the window, his gaze fixed on the darkening landscape below. Twilight swathed all in shadows. ''What do you want from me?''

Finally she had his attention. He stared at her in the fading light, long dark lashes concealing his eyes, his expression curiously hard. There was nothing remotely gentle in his grim features. ''Let's not do this now.''

His English was flawless and yet his tone cut razorsharp. He'd been schooled in the States, she thought blankly, numb from head to toe. ''Are you going to…hurt me?''

She heard the wobble in her voice, the break between words that revealed her fear and exhaustion. He heard it, too, and his firm mouth compressed, flatter, harder. ''I don't hurt women.''

''But you do kidnap them?'' she choked, on the verge of hysteria, her imagination beginning to run away with her. She'd been up twenty-four hours without sleep and she was losing control.

"Only if I'm asked to," he answered as the helicopter dipped. He glanced out the window and nodded with satisfaction. "We're landing. Hold on."

The helicopter touched down. While the pilot worked the controls, her abductor flung the door open and stepped out. "Come," he said, extending a hand to her.

Zoe recoiled from his touch. *"No."*

She couldn't see his face in the darkness but felt his impatience. "It's not a choice, Señorita Collingsworth. *¡Vamanos!*"

Slowly, trembling with fear, she climbed from the helicopter. Her legs were numb and stiff, as if cardboard legs instead of tissue and bone.

The night felt warm, far warmer than she'd expected, and yet she convulsively pressed her thin traveling coat closer to her frame.

Lights shone ahead. Heart pounding, she gazed at the illuminated house and outbuildings. But beyond the immediate circle of light there was only darkness. A world of darkness. Where was she? What did he intend to do?

He moved behind her, reached into the helicopter and lifted out her suitcase and another small traveling bag. His, she thought with a shudder.

Bags out, he shut the helicopter door and immediately the helicopter lifted, rising straight from the ground into the dark starry night.

The whirring blades blew her hair into her eyes and Zoe stumbled backward, trying to escape the noise and rush of air, tripping over the suitcases behind her.

She fell backward. Hands reached out to break her fall.

She felt the hard pressure of his body, felt his hands tighten on her as he placed her on her feet.

Immediately, she pulled away, and yet that split second of contact was more than she could bear. In that split second she'd felt his strength and heat penetrate her coat, penetrate her skin, penetrate all the way into her bones. He was hard and unyielding. Just that brief contact left her burned.

Bruised.

God help me, she silently prayed, *get me home safe.*

Hand shaking, she pushed a fistful of hair from her eyes. Her hair clip had fallen out, and the helicopter blades had blown the long heavy mass free. She felt blown to bits.

Physically. Emotionally.

"This way," he said roughly, touching her elbow.

This second touch was worse than the first. Zoe jerked, muscles snapping, spring-loaded. The sudden stiffening of her body hurt.

Every time he touched her she shuddered. Every time he touched her she burned.

The noise of the helicopter began to fade. The warm night air wrapped around her. "What happens now?" she asked, drawing herself tall, bringing herself to her full five-ten height. It didn't do much good. He was still far taller, larger. He had to be well over six foot three, maybe six-four. He was built strong, too, thickly muscled like an American football star, but in his black coat, black shirt, black trousers he could have been from the Mafia.

"We go inside. We'll have dinner. You'll go to your room for the night."

He made it sound almost civilized. Which should have reassured her, but she wasn't reassured, not by a long shot. She'd heard that some of the most violent men were also the most sophisticated. He could be toying with her before—

Stop it!

You have to stop thinking like this. You can't let your imagination do this to you. You'll just drive yourself crazy.

There were too many unknowns, too many terrifying possibilities. She had to stay calm, had to keep a cool head, as her father used to say. Her father had been a master of cool heads.

She swallowed the lump of panic filling her throat. "Okay. Dinner sounds good." She'd take this step by step, moment by moment. She'd get through this. One way or another.

He picked up her suitcase and his bag and headed toward the house, leaving her to follow. But she couldn't follow, not immediately. How could she just go in there, how could she walk into that house on her own accord?

Zoe stood where he'd left her, turned to face the cement pad, felt the night air surround her. The land was flat and open, with only a cluster of trees in the distance. Nothing loomed on the horizon. No mountains. No lights from a town. Just flat, empty space.

The pampas, she whispered to herself, remembering the postcards Daisy had sent her.

The Galván *estancia* was on the pampas, too. Perhaps she was close to Daisy, closer than either of them knew.

She turned back to face the house with the glow of yellow light. What to do now?

He was waiting for her at the door. She started toward him then stopped. She could feel his impatience and it frightened her. What would happen once she entered the house?

He waited another moment before shrugging and disappearing from view. After a long moment Zoe forced herself to continue.

Climbing the front steps, she arrived at the front door. The dark wood door remained open. The man reappeared.

He'd removed his coat and unbuttoned his dark shirt. A muscle in his jaw jumped as her eyes met his. His eyes were lighter than she'd thought, his eyebrows straight and very black, but it was his nose that dominated his face. His nose was bent, beaked in two places. There was a small scar at the bridge, and another scar at the edge of his square chin. His face looked as though it'd been smashed silly a half dozen times.

A street boxer. A thug.

Zoe's throat constricted. She swallowed hard, terror making her limbs feel like thin splinters of glass.

''You're coming in then?'' he said.

Her throat worked and she dug her fists against her ribs to stop her shaking. It nearly killed her to force sound through her throat. ''You don't care if I stay outside?''

"You can do whatever you want now that you're here."

"I can?"

"There's no phone line here, no outside communication at all. No visitors, no roads, no disturbances, no interruptions. You're safe."

Hot tears pricked her eyes and she ground her teeth together. "I'm *safe?*"

He reached out to touch the side of her neck, just below her jawbone, his fingers trailing across the soft skin left exposed by her turtleneck. "Perfectly safe."

She quivered and jerked at the hot painful touch. "Is there no one else here?"

"Just an elderly servant, but she doesn't speak English and won't bother you."

He lifted his finger from her neck and she felt as though he'd split her in two. The touch had been light and yet he'd lit a bomb inside her skin, heat exploding in her middle, fire racing through her veins. It was the most shocking touch and she wanted to cry out loud, overwhelmed by the intensity of her response.

"Come inside. You're tired."

"I'm afraid."

His dark head tilted. "Of?"

His deep voice was pitched so low that it throbbed within her, a soft but distinct vibration that left her humming. She hated him, feared him, and yet he was strangely charismatic, too. *Of everything that could happen,* she wanted to answer, but she didn't say it. Wouldn't say it.

He must have read her thoughts because he smiled

faintly. "Think of it as an adventure." Then he moved aside, stepping back to allow her to pass.

An adventure? He must be mad.

Yet his peculiar dark-light eyes held hers, and he waited, neither speaking nor rushing her. He was going to let her choose. He was going to put the next move on her.

What should she do? Stay outside in the darkness, on the endless pampas, or go into the warm yellow glow of the house?

With her heart thudding, she stepped inside.

Lazaro spotted Zoe Collingsworth the moment she stepped from the jet-way at the airport earlier in the afternoon. Young, blond, beautiful, she was the epitome of Argentine beauty. His narrowed gaze had followed her movements as she rummaged in her leather handbag for dark sunglasses.

Her hand had shook as she'd propped the tortoiseshell glasses on her small, straight nose. She could have been a Hollywood starlet. Her sweater's high funnel neck stopped just short of her chin, accenting her smooth, creamy jaw and the long tumble of golden hair.

Lazaro could see that the men in the airport waiting area were already projecting their fantasies onto her. They saw what they wanted to see, the full breasts beneath the thin black sweater and the very feminine hips in wool trousers the color of rich caramel. They were admiring her hair, too, wondering if the glorious color was natural.

It was natural. Her hair was like her sister Daisy's,

only more golden. In fact, the two of them looked remarkably similar.

Only two years after marrying Count Dante Galván, Daisy was already considered a great beauty in Argentina's elite social circles, but Zoe had a different beauty than Daisy's…a softer beauty.

Lazaro shut the door to the ranch house but didn't bother locking it. No point in locks. There was nowhere for Zoe to go.

He watched her now as she took a step into the hall, her blue eyes wide, and apprehensive, the irises more lavender than sapphire. She scanned the interior, as if searching for a hidden door or a secret torture chamber.

"There's nothing sinister here," he said calmly. "No knives, guns, whips, chains. Just a simple ranch house."

Her chin lifted, her full lips trembled, but she pressed them together. "Have you sent a ransom note already?"

"No."

She blinked, long black lashes sweeping down, brushing the high elegant curve of her cheekbone before looking up again. She was so young. Nearly twelve years younger than he. A lifetime between them.

The age difference should have killed his attraction. It didn't.

Ever since she'd stepped from the jet-way this afternoon, his gut had ached, his body throbbing. His response to her stunned him. It was such a primitive reaction, so fiercely and purely physical that he felt raw on the inside. Barely controlled.

The desire was there even now and his body tightened yet again, his black wool slacks growing snug, confining.

He felt hungry. Like a prehistoric creature brought back from the dead. Something about her made him crave her, made him feel ravenous. Ruthless.

He wanted to feel her, taste her, possess her. And in a distant part of his brain he knew he would. Someday.

When he'd crushed the Galváns.

When he'd had his revenge.

But this wasn't the time. Right now she was exhausted and afraid, and she was a guest in his house.

"Let me take your coat," he said, softening the edge to his voice, knowing he had a hard voice, and a brusque manner. He wasn't known for his sensitivity, or civility.

He extended a hand for her coat but she took a frightened step back.

Zoe nearly screamed when his hand reached out. She couldn't let him touch her again. She couldn't let him anywhere near her, feeling trapped, helpless, far too vulnerable. Again she was reminded of his height, his size. There was something about him that exuded strength, not just in terms of muscle, but control…power.

She pressed her thin coat more tightly to her body. "I'd like to keep my coat."

His heavy eyebrows lifted. "You'll get it back."

He was making fun of her. Heat banded across her cheekbones and she lifted her chin. ''I'm cold.''

''Come closer to the fire then. It should warm you.''

He led her from the wide high-ceiling hall into a surprisingly spacious sitting room, the dark-beamed ceiling as rustic as the floor-to-ceiling stone fireplace. Yet the furnishings were luxurious, from the vibrant scarlet and gold rug covering the wood-planked floor to the deep plush sofas and chairs clustered in small groupings. The artwork on the walls were all massive canvases, oversize oil paintings in vivid brush-strokes—electric blue, blood red, hot yellow.

This was no simple ranch house.

Zoe moved past the wrought-iron and leather coffee table with its stacks of books toward the fire. Her legs felt brittle, her muscles taut.

With a fleeting glance at the bookcases behind her, she reached out to the stone hearth, trembling fingers spread wide to capture the fire's heat.

Kidnapped, she repeated silently, she'd been kidnapped. It still hadn't completely sunk in. Would it ever?

She remembered disembarking the plane, remembered filing out of the jet-way with the other passengers and entering the gate area to discover a waiting throng.

She remembered scanning the crowd, looking for Dante, or a driver. Dante had promised someone would be there to meet her. But she didn't see Dante, or anyone holding a sign. There were mothers and young children, businessmen in suits on cell phones, elderly seniors in wheelchairs but no one for her.

Her eyes had suddenly watered as she felt a pang of loss. Normally something like this wouldn't upset her, but it hadn't been a normal month. Her father was getting so much worse. He seemed to have forgotten everything now and it was awful watching him fade before her eyes. He'd been a smart man, and a loving man, always generous with others.

Her eyes continued to well with tears and she dug in her shoulder bag for her sunglasses. She'd cried most of the flight, and the oversize black sunglasses had come in handy then, too. The truth was, she'd cried so much in the last month she should be out of tears, but somehow the tears just kept coming.

Sunglasses in place she felt better. She took a deep breath and tried to focus on the positives. She was here to see Daisy. Soon she'd be reunited with her sister. Things would be better once they were together.

It was at that very moment when he approached her, the man in the black coat and shirt, the unsmiling man with a piercing gaze and a strong beaked nose.

"Miss Collingsworth?" he'd said, his voice impossibly deep, so deep she'd blinked behind her sunglasses as she let his voice sink into her, tangible and real.

Zoe recalled that her travel guide said Argentine men—a blend of Latin passion and European sophistication—were lethally attractive and while she wouldn't call this man classically handsome, he was arresting...no, intriguing, in a primitive sort of way.

"I'm Zoe," she'd answered, her heart doing a strange double beat. She'd been up all night and was overly tired. She'd never traveled out of Kentucky before and had felt ambivalent emotions about the trip to Argentina. She wanted to see Daisy, yet she hated putting her father in a nursing home. True, he wouldn't stay there long, just the two weeks she was in Argentina, but it had been awful driving him there, awful leaving him there.

"Do you have any bags?" the man asked.

"Just one," she answered. "It's a large case so I checked it through."

His dark head inclined, his glossy blue-black hair cut short. "If you give me your tag, I'll get it for you."

His hand stretched toward her, his palm wide, fingers long, well-shaped. He fit his skin somehow. He looked comfortable with himself and she'd given him the tag. They went to baggage claim and he lifted the heavy case off the carousel as though it weighed nothing. A limousine was waiting for them outside baggage claim and they drove straight to the helicopter pad.

It wasn't until they were in midair and she'd begun to ask questions about Daisy and her pregnancy, about the Galván *estancia,* about life on the pampas that he'd told her to stop talking.

Actually, what he'd said was, *Be quiet, do as you're told, and everything will be fine.*

Zoe drew a deep breath and stared at the fire with its red and gold dancing flames.

She was shaking again, more violently now than

earlier, and with each uneven breath she could smell the acrid scent of burning wood and smoke, yet the heat wasn't enough. She couldn't stop shivering. Couldn't control her nerves.

She heard him walk behind her, heard the clink of glass, the slosh of liquid, another clink. He was pouring himself a drink. What kind of kidnapper embraced leather books, modern art and brandy decanters? *What kind of man was he?*

Zoe battled her fear. There had to be a good explanation. People didn't just abduct other people without having a purpose, a plan.

"Drink this."

His cool hard voice sliced into her thoughts, drawing her gaze up, from the fire to his chiseled features, his expression inexplicably grim. "I don't drink."

"It'll warm you."

She glanced at the balloon-shaped brandy glass in his hand, quarter filled with amber liquid, and shrank from him. "I don't like the taste."

"I didn't use to like it much when I was your age, either." He continued to hold the glass out to her. "You're shivering. It'll help. Trust me."

Trust him? He was the last man she'd ever trust. He'd taken her from Daisy, Dante, from the reunion she'd long anticipated. Her throat threatened to seal closed, her temper rising as her anger got the best of her.

She turned on him, arms bundled across her chest. "Who are you, anyway? I don't even know your name."

"Lazaro Herrera."

The name rolled off his tongue, fluid, complex, sensual. The r's trilled, the z was accented, the vowels so rich and smoky they could have been aged whiskey.

Lazaro Herrera.

It was a name that fit him, a name that echoed of strength and muscle and power. "I think I'll take that drink," she whispered.

His fingers brushed hers as he handed her the glass. "Sip it. Slowly."

His skin was warm yet his touch scalded her. She nearly dropped the glass. "Why are you doing this?"

He shrugged, a vague shift of his massive shoulders. "I have reasons."

"But what did I do? You don't even know me."

"This isn't about you."

"Then what is it about?" Her voice had risen.

"Revenge."

CHAPTER TWO

SHE stared at him aghast, the only sound in the house the crackle and pop of the fire.

Zoe shook so badly that brandy came sloshing up and over the rim of her glass. Her mouth felt parched. It tasted ridiculously like cotton. She swallowed roughly, trying to think of something—anything—to say.

Revenge. Revenge against...*whom?*

But she couldn't ask because she knew she wasn't prepared for the truth, wasn't prepared to hear the words he'd say. She knew somehow that his answer would impact Daisy, it had to impact Daisy because Daisy had married here, into the Argentine aristocracy and Daisy had become part of this world, this culture, this other life.

Sick at heart, Zoe lifted the balloon-shaped glass to her lips and took a small sip. The brandy felt cool in her mouth then turned hot as she swallowed. The warmth hit her stomach and finally seeped into her limbs.

Lazaro Herrera was right about one thing. The liquor did help. It bolstered her courage. She wrapped her hands around the glass. "Does this have to do with the Galváns?"

"You're very perceptive."

"You want money?"

"Doesn't everyone?"

But his answer didn't ring true, nor did his sarcasm. There was something else driving him and she needed to understand, needed to know so she could protect Daisy. "Does Dante know about this yet?"

"He should."

She stared down into her brandy, trying to calm herself. She couldn't help Daisy if she lost her head. "My sister, Dante's wife, is pregnant."

"I know."

"Please don't hurt Daisy." Her voice had thickened. The words came out hoarse. She felt the back of her eyes sting, gritty tears welling. "She's had several miscarriages and it's been devastating for her. She can't lose this baby."

He stared at her, his silver-gray eyes shuttered. "I have no desire to hurt her."

"But you will." Zoe didn't know how she knew, but she knew and it made her furious. Lazaro Herrera would destroy her family and never look back.

"Things happen in life—"

"No," she burst out, gripping the glass tightly. "You're doing this, you're creating this."

"It's complicated, *corazón*. Life has never been easy."

He was sidestepping the issue, turning the argument around, and it infuriated her. She took a step toward him, her slim body rigid with tension. Her family had been through so much in the past couple of years. They'd struggled and suffered and finally, just when Daisy found some happiness, this man threatened to take it away.

"Of course life is difficult. It's full of pain and sorrow and loss, but it's also full of joy and love—" she broke off, realizing she was dangerously close to tears, and swallowed hard. "Don't hurt my sister. You can't. I won't let you."

He wouldn't acknowledge what she'd said. He ignored her fury. "You're still shivering. You need a hot bath."

"I don't want a hot bath. I don't want anything from you. Not now, not ever."

His gaze swept her face. Her face felt hot in places. She knew her cheeks were flushed and her eyes glowed overbright.

"It doesn't exactly work that way," he said at last. "You are my guest here. This is my house. We will be together virtually night and day the next several weeks. I suggest you get used to my company. Quickly."

He walked out.

Zoe stood there for several moments before her muscles twitched to life. Slowly she placed the half-full brandy glass on the coffee table before wiping her damp palms on the sides of her pale traveling coat.

She remembered when she boarded the flight yesterday evening how chic she'd thought she'd looked in the long thin cream coat and cream-colored cowboy boots. She and Daisy had grown up in boots. Just like they'd grown up in the saddle, working the farm. She might look fragile, but there was nothing fragile about her.

Just her feelings, maybe.

Zoe pushed up her coat sleeve and looked at her wristwatch. Almost seven-thirty. She'd arrived in Buenos Aires over six hours ago. Daisy must be frantic.

Forehead furrowing, Zoe looked about for a phone. He'd said there was no phone but she didn't believe him. Everyone had phones these days. She'd look for a phone jack first. The phone jack would be a dead giveaway that he'd merely unplugged the phone and hidden it away. She'd find the phone and call for help first chance possible.

"Your bath is ready."

·Lazaro had returned and he stood in the doorway. He'd changed into dark slacks and a thick dark sweater. The dense weave of the sweater flattered his hard features, softening his long crooked nose and square chin.

He almost looked human.

Almost.

"I'm not going to take a bath. I'm not going to stay here." She left the fire, walked swiftly from the living room to the hall, holding her breath as she moved past him.

She half expected him to stop her as she reached for the door but he didn't move. He didn't even bat an eyelash as she yanked the heavy door open.

"It's a long walk to town," he said mildly. "And very dark. There aren't any streetlights on the pampas."

She gripped the doorknob, hating him, hating his reasonable tone. "I've been in the country before."

"Then you know how confusing it gets to walk

without landmarks, without roads, without any sign of human life.''

''Your ranch can't be that remote.''

His eyebrows merely lifted.

''I'm sure there's *something* out there,'' she insisted.

''Sheep. Cows. Deer—''

''Not very frightening.''

''Jaguars, pumas, cougars.''

Zoe swallowed hard. ''You're lying.''

''I wouldn't lie to you.''

''All you've done is lie to me,'' she flung back at him, turning to face him, hand still tight on the iron doorknob.

''I haven't lied to you yet—''

''At the airport you asked me if I was Zoe Collingsworth—''

''And you said yes.'' A humongous brown moth flit from the front porch light into the hall. Lazaro moved toward Zoe and gently but firmly closed the door. ''I asked you for your baggage tag and you gave it to me. You came with me, Zoe. Happily. Willingly. Immediately.''

Tears of shock and shame filled her eyes. ''You let me think you worked for Dante!''

''And I do.''

Zoe fell back, leaned against the closed door. She pressed her palms to the surface. ''You *what?*''

''I work for your brother-in-law. I work for Dante Galván.''

She couldn't have heard him right. Something had

to be wrong with her head or her ears. "What can you possibly do for him?"

"Everything."

Lazaro's lips had twisted and his cynical smile filled her with fresh horror. She closed her eyes and pressed a fist between her eyebrows, pressing at the throbbing in her head. This was crazy. Worse than crazy. "Please explain what you mean by *everything*," she choked, unable to look at him. "Are you some kind of Boy Friday?"

"Hardly. I'm the president of Galván Enterprises."

Her head jerked up, eyes opening. "But Dante's the president."

"Dante is the chief executive officer. I run day-to-day operations."

"Since when?"

"Since two years ago."

"But—"

"Enough. I don't want to discuss this anymore, not with you swaying on your feet. You're tired, you need to bathe, eat, relax. Believe me, we'll have plenty of time to talk later."

He turned away but she didn't follow. "How much time?" she called after him.

He stopped walking, slowly faced her. "What?"

"You said we'd have plenty of time to talk later. I want to know how much time it is. How long do you intend to keep me here?"

"Depends. It could be a week, could be two, but if I were you, I'd plan on two."

She opened her mouth to protest but he'd already

turned the corner and disappeared down another hall-
way into a different part of the house.

Zoe followed much more slowly, passing through
a darkened bedroom into a large luxurious bathroom.
It was the most sumptuous bath she'd ever seen. The
floor, walls, bath—even the shower stall itself—were
covered in a gorgeous red marble. The sink and bath-
tub were made of gold, the tub was oversize, at least
big enough for two people, and already filled with
water.

Lazaro left her to undress, but Zoe couldn't.

She sank to the edge of the tub, sat on the wide
surround and stared at the steamy water. Pools of
scented oil floated on the water surface. He'd put
something in there, something that smelled rich, com-
forting.

She couldn't reconcile anything he'd told her.

Minutes passed and still she didn't move, couldn't
move.

A knock sounded on the outside of the bathroom
door. She didn't answer and the knob turned, the door
slowly opened.

"Are you all right?" Lazaro's voice came from the
shadows outside the door.

What a question! Was she all right?

No, she wasn't all right, she was anything but all
right. Her father was dying. Her sister was on bedrest
with a difficult pregnancy. She'd been proposed to by
an old family friend who was more old than friend.
All right? No, Zoe concluded silently, savagely, she
was most definitely *not* all right.

Lazaro stepped inside the bath and looked at her.

She hadn't moved, he saw, and he gave his head a small imperceptible shake. He felt sympathy for her and it was the last emotion he wanted to feel.

Moving toward her, he crouched down in front of her. "You're getting yourself all worked up. Nothing bad is going to happen to you. Nothing bad will happen to Daisy, either. I promise."

Her mouth quivered. Her eyes searched his, her lashes damp, matted. "How can I trust you?"

"I don't know." He fought the urge to touch her, fought the desire to reach out and cup her cheek. Her skin looked so soft, so tender. Like her heart, he thought, she was soft. She shouldn't have ever been exposed to a man like him.

This was Dante's doing.

In Dante's determination to protect Daisy, he'd exposed Zoe, rendered her vulnerable.

Lazaro felt a tightness in his chest, anger and revulsion. He'd felt this same anger and revulsion nearly all his life. The dirty, barefoot street kid outside the store window looking in. To want something and be denied, not just once, but your entire life…

He, the outcast, the untouchable, had climbed the social ladder but he hadn't forgotten and he hadn't forgiven. If anything, the rage burned hotter, brighter, and he was more determined than ever to take what was rightfully his. To seize life—opportunity—and shake it by the throat.

Yet looking at young Zoe Collingsworth he realized all over again how ruthless he'd become, how hard and cruel.

He saw her hands balled in her lap. She was pressing her nails into her palms, the bare nails digging deep, breaking the skin.

"Give me your hand," he said quietly.

She shook her head.

"Give me your hand," he repeated.

He could see the fear in her eyes, as well as the uncertainty. She didn't know what to expect, didn't know what he wanted with her. Truthfully, he wasn't entirely sure, either. Sex, maybe. But there was something else, something he couldn't define but powerful, intoxicating. He was drawn to her. Which would only worsen Dante's situation.

He waited for her hand and slowly she slipped her palm onto his. His fingers wrapped around hers, his hand holding hers firmly, securely.

"You are safe with me, Zoe. My fight is not with you. Trust me on this."

Every time he touched her, it happened, she thought wildly. Heat, energy, pleasure. His touch was unlike any touch she'd ever known. There was something in his skin, something warmer, stronger, more real.

Zoe stared at his hand, felt the heat and the ripple of delicious sensation surge through her, hand to heart, heart to belly, belly to legs.

Her heart slowed, her body felt liquid, bones melting, even as her senses became quivery and alert.

"Daisy's everything to me," she said, mesmerized by the back of his hand, with the burnished-gold skin and the wide strong bones of his wrist. "She practically raised me. She gave up college for me—"

Suddenly he leaned forward, his dark head blocking light and she knew he was going to kiss her. It was as though she'd known from the very first moment she'd met him that this would happen, that this kiss was destined to happen.

His mouth brushed hers. It was a fleeting kiss, a kiss so light her heart ached and tears pricked the backs of her eyes all over again. She could feel his breath against her cheek, smell the sweetness and subtle spice of his cologne. He was big and strong and dark, and yet he smelled of light, sunshine, like meadow grass and flowers after an early summer rain.

His lips barely grazed hers a second time. His mouth slid over her lips to the corner of her mouth. "I will try my best to protect your sister from this, too."

It wasn't the same promise he'd made her. She was afraid to ask, but she had to. "What about Dante?"

Lazaro stiffened. "What about Dante?"

His voice had hardened, the tone turning cold. He didn't like Dante. "This is about Dante."

"Yes."

This was about Dante.

Zoe rushed from beneath his arm, fled to the far side of the red marble bathroom.

This was about Dante. He'd kidnapped her to hurt Dante. He'd done this to make Dante suffer.

But she adored Dante. He was the big brother she'd never had. He'd saved their farm, fallen in love with Daisy, had taken care of their father. Dante was the answer to the Collingsworths's prayers.

She felt sick, and cold again, deeply cold, as though fear and pain had settled all the way into the marrow of her bones. Pointing to the door, Zoe ordered Lazaro out. "Go."

He slowly stood, rising to his full height. In the dimmed light his cheekbones looked like angular slashes above his full mouth. His broken nose shadowed his blunt chin. "Someday you will understand."

"I will never understand. Dante is a good man. He's the most generous man I know."

"You don't know the full story."

"Get out." She turned her back on him, wrapped her arms across her chest.

He crossed to the door. "No matter what happens, I will keep my promise to you."

In the bath Zoe soaped and scrubbed, feeling sullied after the trip, the abduction, the kiss. She didn't understand how she could feel so many intensely conflicting emotions. She was afraid of Lazaro Herrera and yet intrigued.

Toweling off, Zoe knew she had to act to get word to Dante and Daisy, knew time was of the essence. She'd look for that phone as soon as she could.

Dry and wrapped in a robe, she faced the open closet in her adjoining bedroom. Someone had unpacked for her. She couldn't imagine it was Lazaro.

Zoe didn't like feeling naked in this strange house and dressed quickly, putting on comfortable jeans and a well-washed yellow sweatshirt. She'd just started to put on socks and sneakers when a knock sounded at the door.

Opening the door, Zoe discovered a tiny old woman, no taller than five feet, with gray-streaked hair and an extremely wrinkled olive-complexioned face. "Hello."

"*¡Vamanos!*" The unsmiling old woman crossed her hands over her stomach. Her voice sounded sharp. *"La cena."*

Definitely not a warm welcome. "I'm sorry, I don't understand," Zoe answered slowly in English. "I don't speak Spanish."

"La cena. La comida."

"I'm sorry, I don't understand."

The older woman exhaled noisily, tossed up her hands. *"¿Que dice?"*

"I…I don't know what you want me to do. I don't speak Spanish."

"¿Que?"

"Señor Herrera. Ask Señor Herrera, *sí?*"

The elderly woman muttered something beneath her breath and stalked off. She made it halfway down the hall before turning around.

With short, curt gestures she motioned to her mouth, and opened and shut her mouth in an exaggerated chewing motion. *"La comida. La cena. La cena."*

Understanding dawned. *"La cena."* Food, dinner, Zoe finally got it. But that didn't mean she was going to rush on out and eat. Who wanted to be invited to dinner like that?

Zoe shut her door and it slammed closed far harder than she intended. Wincing, she climbed on her bed, grabbed a pillow and buried her face in the pillow where she let out a muffled scream of frustration.

This was a nightmare.

She couldn't stay here. Nothing made sense. Everything was off kilter, from the brandy to the marble bathroom to the kiss. She felt lost…confused.

Her door banged open less than two minutes after she'd slammed it shut.

"¡Por Dios! What happened?" Lazaro demanded from the doorway. "I've never seen Luz so upset."

"Luz?"

"My housekeeper." He braced his hands on his hips, indignation written all over his hard, dark features. "What did you say to her?"

"Nothing."

"Yet clearly you've offended her."

Zoe mashed the pillow between her hands, squeezing the pillow into a ball. "You've got to be joking."

"No. She said you spit in her face and slammed the door. I heard the door slam, too."

Zoe flushed. "I didn't spit. I wouldn't spit. That's rude." She swallowed hard. "And I didn't mean to slam the door. It closed harder than I expected."

He stared at her for a long moment, his jaw tight, his mouth compressed. He seemed to be considering her, the situation, Luz's version of events. *"Que joda,"* he ground out after a moment.

"What did you say?"

"I said, what a nuisance. You don't want dinner, fine. Stay in your room. But I'm not going to send special trays to you. There is a dining room in this house, and a very nice antique table with matching chairs. If you want to go to bed hungry, that's your choice. If you want to eat, you know where I—and the food—will be."

He knew she wouldn't join him for dinner and he didn't have dinner held. It didn't bother him eating alone in the elegant dining room, either. He almost always ate alone, and had ever since his mother died when he was seven.

He used to think it was poverty that killed her. The two of them were always hungry, and despite the fact that she worked every job she could secure, there never seemed to be enough money to get them off the streets.

Luz entered the dining room, reached for his plate, saw that he'd barely made a dent in his dinner. "Not hungry?" she asked sharply, her wrinkled brow doubly lined with concern.

Luz had befriended his mother before she died. Luz had been poorer than his mother, too, and yet she had fire, and a fierce spirit which made her fight back against those who would oppress her. She'd tried to teach his young mother, Sabana, to stand up to the aristocratic Galváns but his mother was terrified of the powerful Galván family.

"I'll have coffee and something light later," he said, leaning back so she could clear his place.

Luz held the plate in her hands. "Who is she, the girl?"

"A friend of a friend."

Luz made a rough clucking sound. "The truth."

"It's half truth, and that's enough for you to know." Lazaro pushed away from the table. "Thank you for dinner."

He walked out, headed for the living room and discovered the fire had burned low. Sitting down on the couch, he put his feet on the massive iron and wood coffee table and stared into the glowing embers.

He'd built this house for his mother. Of course she'd been gone nearly twenty-five years when he had the plans drawn and the house finished, but the attention to detail had been for her, in honor of her. He'd insisted on the best of everything. Crystal chandeliers, silk window hangings, marble bathrooms, French antiques.

She'd been a beautiful girl when Count Tino Galván took her against her will. Just seventeen. Not even out of high school.

But taking her innocence hadn't been enough for Count Galván. After he'd hurt her, Tino Galván had Sabana sent away, exiled to a remote Patagonia village where she delivered her son alone. The Galváns had hoped the baby wouldn't survive.

But Lazaro had.

Since his mother died, he lived for but one thing. Revenge. Revenge on those who hurt his mother, and revenge on those who'd shut their doors on him.

Zoe went to bed hungry and woke up ravenous at three in the morning. Between the time change and the growling of her stomach, she couldn't fall back to sleep. Lying in bed awake, her thoughts quickly turned to Daisy. Daisy would be worried sick and Zoe knew she had to reach her sister as soon as possible and reassure her everything was fine.

She also needed to alert Dante to the danger Lazaro posed, without getting Daisy involved.

Throwing back the bedcovers, Zoe slid out from

between the warm sheets and reached for her thin white cotton robe that matched the pink-sprigged nightgown.

It was a girlish set, something she'd had forever and yet refused to part with despite the cotton wearing thin and the rosebuds fading to peach and cream. The sleep set had been a gift from her dad years ago. Daisy got one like it, only hers had been blue.

Opening her bedroom door, she peered down the darkened hall. She wasn't sure where to begin searching for a phone. She knew there had to be one somewhere, and not just a phone, but a fax, a modem, a cell phone. Lazaro Herrera had to communicate with the outside world somehow.

In the living room, Zoe crept on her hands and knees along the baseboards, searching for a hidden phone jack, running her fingers along the edge of plaster wall and wood base. She worked her way around the living room before moving to the bookcase where she inspected each shelf.

Nothing. At least not yet.

From living room to hall, hall to the cavernous kitchen, around the kitchen islands and huge rough-hewn pillars to the dining room.

She'd just finished circling the circumference of the dark dining room when she heard a cough behind her.

"Lose something, Zoe?"

"No." She rose and brushed off her hands. It was so dark she could hardly see him but she felt him, felt his energy from ten feet away.

A little bit of moonlight fell through the window,

illuminating his profile. "You're not cleaning, are you? Luz wouldn't like it."

"I'm not cleaning."

"Then what are you doing creeping around the house at three-thirty in the morning?"

A long lock of hair fell forward, brushing her cheek, and she tucked it behind her ear. "You know what I'm doing. You know what I want."

"You won't find a phone."

"Not even a computer jack?"

"I've taken precautions. I've been quite thorough."

"Let me go."

"No."

"I'll go back to Kentucky, I'll call Daisy and tell her I changed my mind about coming out—"

"No."

She felt dangerously close to losing it, to screaming and crying and begging. "This isn't fair."

"But we've already discussed this, and we know life isn't always fair. If life was fair your mother wouldn't have died after your birth. If life was fair your father wouldn't have Alzheimer's. If life was fair your only sister wouldn't have moved halfway around the world leaving you to take care of your sick father—"

"How…how…do you know all that?"

"This wasn't a random abduction, Zoe. I made sure I knew what I was doing." He flicked on the dining room light fixture, a large iron and crystal chandelier. "Now go back to bed and get some sleep. You need it. We both need it."

In a white T-shirt and loose black cotton pajama
pants with his black hair ruffled, he looked incredibly
male. And human. He looked like a man that knew
all about women. He looked like a man that knew
how to use his hands, his body and his mouth.

Heat seeped through Zoe's limbs, color sweeping
her cheeks. She hated that she could find him physically attractive when his character was so appalling.
He was awful, cruel, twisted. ''I hate you.''

She hadn't meant to say it. But the words slipped
out anyway.

His dark head merely inclined and his beautiful lips
shaped into a small shadow of a smile. ''I know.''

CHAPTER THREE

THE helicopter that carried Lazaro off just before dawn, leaving Zoe alone with Luz for the next three days, finally returned.

Zoe heard the buzzing of the blades in her sleep, heard the whine grow louder and louder until the helicopter sounded as though it had landed in the middle of Luz's herb garden.

So he was back.

She squeezed her eyes more tightly closed, wishing her heart wasn't flopping around inside her.

She was glad. How could she be glad? She hated him.

I do, she firmly told herself, opening her eyes and staring at the dark-beamed ceiling. She'd grown to like the yellow plaster walls in her bedroom that contrasted with the dark beams. The tapestry cover on her bed was woven in shades of yellow, deep rose and green.

Everything was so different in this house, so different from the way she'd grown up. Four days after arriving here, she still felt completely alien.

Luz didn't help much, either. The housekeeper-cook was less than hospitable, taking every possible opportunity to shut a door in Zoe's face, serve cold food, ignore Zoe's halting questions.

A knock sounded on the door just seconds before

the door opened. Luz entered the bedroom with a tray and her now familiar glare of disapproval. No, Zoe thought, sitting up in bed, relations hadn't exactly warmed up between the two of them.

"Café," Luz announced curtly, setting the tray on the edge of the bed with just enough force to slosh coffee up and over the rim of the cup.

Somehow Zoe knew the coffee would be luke-warm, too. "Thank you," she answered stiffly.

"You might try *'gracias,'*" a voice said from the doorway. "Luz would at least understand your thanks."

And here he was, freshly returned from battle. Or civilization. Or wherever he'd gone. Her temper grew to near bursting point, and she dragged the covers higher against her chest as if she could control her anger. "You're back."

"Happy to see me?"

"No."

His cool silver eyes flashed and she saw a hint of amusement and something else in the pewter depths. He moved to the foot of her bed and stood, arms folded, eyes narrowed in appraisal. "You're still in bed. It's almost noon."

He made her feel difficult, unreasonable. "I didn't know I had social obligations," she answered tersely. But this was his problem, not hers. He was the one who kidnapped her. He was the one who dumped her here and flew away, back to Buenos Aires, because that's where she suspected he'd gone.

Back to work.

With Dante.

"Did you see him?" she asked, fingers tightly stretching the linen.

"See who?"

Lazaro was playing dumb. He knew perfectly well who she meant. Zoe's chest hurt as she drew a deep breath, fighting for patience as well as control. "Dante."

"Oh." Lazaro smiled lazily, and walking around the foot of the bed, approached her side. "Yes. I did see him, but then as I've already told you, I work with him. Closely."

The word *closely* hung there between them, strange, rather sinister. The word implied trust, intimacy, safety.

It still stunned her to think that Dante's confidant, his most senior in command, intended to betray him.

Like Iago and Othello, she thought, and she knew the tragic outcome there. Zoe suppressed a shiver. "Does he know I'm here?"

"Yes."

Lazaro stood so close to the bed that he could touch Zoe with the tips of his fingers if he wanted.

And he wanted to. He wanted her more than he'd ever wanted anyone and he didn't know why, or how. It just was. Something about her made him hungry to touch her. From those brief caresses he knew he liked the feel of her and in the past three days he found himself craving her, craving to know her skin, her smell, her taste.

He'd thought she'd looked beautiful in the black turtleneck and sunglasses, and yet now, virtually stripped bare, long blond hair tousled, her delicate features scrubbed of all makeup, she looked even more astonishing. Beautiful and sweet. Heart-breakingly innocent, too.

He watched her eyes close, her cheeks pale. She took a deep, shuddering breath before opening her eyes again. "What do you want from him?"

"I've already told you."

"Revenge," she spit back, as if unable to stomach such a word, much less the concept.

"Exactly."

Her face lifted, her lavender eyes wide, incomprehensible. "But for what? Revenge against what?"

"The Galváns."

She drew the sheet higher, tighter, so that it pressed against her breasts, outlining the rise and swell, the delicate ridge of nipple. "But you work for the Galváns, you are president of their corporation."

"Yes."

"You must have spent years working to get where you are."

"Nearly thirteen."

"So…why hurt them? Why destroy your career?"

He slid the tray over and sat down on the mattress next to her. She shuddered as he sat down. But she wasn't afraid of him. She was afraid of the attraction.

Good girl. Smart girl. She should be afraid. He'd never felt anything so powerful in his life.

"My career," he said carefully, placing a hand on the bed, near her thigh, drawing the cover taut across the tone muscle, "has but one focus, and one purpose. To destroy the Galváns."

Zoe had never punched anyone in her life. She'd

never raised a hand, made a fist, used physical violence of any sort. But suddenly she'd closed her fingers, wrapped her thumb over her knuckles and slammed her fist into his chest, in the hollow at his breastbone. It hurt when she struck him and it wasn't even a fierce blow, more pathetic than anything, and he, she noticed through the tears filling her eyes, didn't even flinch.

"How can you be so cruel?" she choked. "How can you care so little about other people?"

He shrugged. "Habit."

"That's a lousy excuse!"

"Blame it on my family then."

"Your family?" Zoe flung her head back, unshed tears glittering in her eyes. "And just who is your family?"

"The Galváns."

Zoe felt sick. She felt physically ill, ill to the point that she actually crouched over the toilet in her red-marble bathroom, hugged the sides of the lavatory seat and heaved and heaved—nothing came up—but the tears didn't stop.

He couldn't be Dante's brother.

Half brother, she corrected, but a brother was a brother was a brother.

My God, they had the same dad. They were practically the same age, born just six months apart.

It had all come out, or most of it had come out, and she'd begged him to stop talking but he hadn't, not until he'd filled her head with words that wouldn't go away.

Lazaro had left her room and she'd run in here, to crouch at the lavatory and gag on the horrible awful things he'd said.

How could a brother destroy a brother?

The bathroom door opened. Luz stood there, dark eyes narrow and unfriendly. *"¿La gripe?"* she asked, freshly laundered towels in her arms.

Zoe sat back, wiped her nose and eyes on a crumpled tissue. *"La gripe?"* she repeated dumbly, hating that she couldn't communicate in the slightest with the housekeeper.

Lazaro appeared behind Luz. "The flu," he translated. "She wants to know if you're sick."

At heart, Zoe thought, swallowing hard. "Tell her I'm fine. Just sad."

His light eyes narrowed. "There's no reason for you to be sad. This isn't your problem."

Zoe rose. "Of course it's my problem." She took a step forward, hands balled at her sides, anger making her head light. "He's my family now, too, and if you think I'll stand by while you do whatever it is you intend to do, you're wrong."

"You don't know him."

She took another step, fury growing by the moment. "Maybe you're the one that doesn't know him. Maybe you're the one that just thinks you do."

He lifted a hand, gestured Luz away before reaching out and clasping Zoe lightly around the wrist. He brought her toward him despite her obvious reluctance. "How well do you know him, Zoe?"

His voice had dropped lower, huskier, and it shivered down her spine even as the heat of his hand burned through the skin at her wrist. The heat was the main thing, the most pressing thing. She felt warm from the inside out, warm just touching him, warm from standing so close to him.

Her mouth went dry. Her heart was pounding inside her chest. She touched the tip of her tongue to her upper lip, trying to ease the dryness. "Don't you dare insinuate—"

"Insinuate?" Lazaro softly interrupted, drawing her closer still. "I'm not insinuating anything. I'm telling you. I'm telling you how this is, how this works. You're here because Dante told me to bring you here. This was his idea, *corazón*. His plan."

"No."

"Yes."

"Dante sent the postcard, Dante arranged the airline ticket, Dante ordered me to meet you. He wanted you here."

Horror filled her, horror and cold intrigue. This was the most preposterous thing she'd heard in her life. She knew he was lying yet she wanted to hear the rest. "Why would Dante want me here?"

"To keep you out of trouble."

"But I'm not in trouble!"

Lazaro smiled faintly, grimly, the smile failing to reach his silver eyes. "He thinks you are."

She'd felt as if he'd given her a ferocious one-two blow to the midsection. She hurt badly, hurt all the way through her.

He must have seen her shock because he suddenly clapped his hands on her shoulders. "You need to get outside, breathe some air, maybe take some exercise. You'll feel better, I'm sure.''

"You're lying."

His fingers settled into her collarbone, holding her still. ''I wouldn't lie to you.''

"You'd abduct me, hold me prisoner, but you wouldn't lie? Now there are some admirable ethics.''

His expression hardened, the silver glints in his eyes turning silver-white and frosty. His hands fell away from her shoulders but his posture was ramrod straight. ''We're going to go riding. I suggest you change, unless you intend to ride in your little-girl nightie.''

She'd forgotten she still wore her pink-sprigged nightgown and self-consciously reached up to touch the lace at the neck. ''You think I'd go anywhere with you? You're a liar and a kidnapper—''

"Did you think I was asking you?'' His eyebrows lifted. ''My apologies, then. I wasn't asking, I was telling you. We're going riding. We'll leave in a half hour.''

"No.''

"Sí.'' He hesitated in the doorway, a strange expression on his rugged face. ''You can ride, can't you?''

"Of course I can ride. My family breeds horses.''

"Yes, but that doesn't indicate any level of…*expertise.*''

She felt rather than heard the innuendo as his narrowed gaze slowly traveled the length of her, resting provocatively on her breasts and the vee between her legs. She felt a blush of mortification that he'd study her so thoroughly, and so thoroughly casually. Yet the slow appreciative scrutiny had coiled the nerves in her tummy and made her legs feel wobbly.

"If I chose to ride with you, I'd outride you, but I'm not riding with you. I don't like you, and I don't trust you, and I know Dante would never ever have me kidnapped. He's not that kind of a person. He's loyal and protective and chivalrous—"

"He's also incredibly self-serving. You're here because you pose a danger to Daisy. It's as simple as that. I'm to keep you out of the way until Daisy has her baby." He glanced at his watch, noted the time. "In a half hour, Zoe. Time's ticking."

She felt a small ripple of fear but something in his eyes and smile thrilled her at the same time. He aroused so many conflicting emotions within her. She didn't understand what it was she felt, but it was intense, more intense than anything she'd ever felt before. "And if I'm not there?" she whispered.

She felt his gaze rest on her mouth, her neck, her breasts. A tingling sensation radiated from her nipples out, the areoles tightening, her body responding.

"I'll come for you," he drawled slowly, "and I won't be as charming as I am now."

He moved forward, dropped a kiss on the top of her head. "I'll see you in half an hour."

She wasn't going to go. She'd rot in hell before she went.

But standing beneath the shower, letting the water stream down on her, she couldn't block out Lazaro's voice, couldn't forget the threat, or the poison of his lies.

What he'd told her had to be lies. Dante would never have her kidnapped, or abducted, or whatever one wanted to call it. He wouldn't send airline tickets behind Daisy's back, he wouldn't ask someone to do dirty work for him. He just wasn't that kind of person.

Zoe grabbed the soap, lathered it up and scrubbed the washcloth up and down her arms as if she could somehow wash away the words and lies and awful things said.

Lazaro was trying to upset her, confuse her, knock her off balance. This was part of his plan for revenge. This was his way of creating strife within the family. He was trying to pit them against each other, sister against sister, wife against husband, Collingsworth against Galván. But she wouldn't let him succeed. She wouldn't buy into his games.

She'd beat him at his game.

"Didn't think you were going to come," Lazaro said as Zoe entered the stable twenty minutes later, dressed in riding pants, a white T-shirt and boots.

"You're right. I could use the exercise," she answered coolly, hating how her heart pounded and her limbs felt weak. She'd felt strong until she'd come face-to-face with him again.

What was it about him that made her feel like this? He turned her inside out, made her into a jellyfish. It was incredible. Painful.

Lazaro's lips twisted. "Why don't I believe you?"

"Because you have a big problem with trust."

Lazaro threw back his head, his loose fleece sweatshirt dipping low enough to reveal the curve of his collarbone and his bronze throat, and laughed.

He laughed.

She'd never heard him laugh before; realized he was a man that didn't laugh often.

"Out of the mouths of babes," he said, choking with husky laughter. "Very good, *corazón.*"

She hadn't expected him to look so virile, so rugged. She'd imagined he'd dress in tight cream jodhpurs, high leather boots, a smart collar shirt. Instead he wore faded denims that clung to his muscular thighs, hugged his hips and sat low on his waist. "What does that mean anyway?"

"It's just an endearment."

"An endearment?" She blushed.

In his boots he towered over her, his immense shoulders even larger in the soft dove-gray sweatshirt, a color that made his eyes look like liquid silver, and she found herself staring into them, thinking he had secrets she could only guess at, and that he'd lived things he'd never share.

He was, she thought, fighting a fit of nerves, frighteningly beautiful, frighteningly amoral, and frighteningly sexual. "What kind of endearment?" she persisted huskily.

"*Corazón* means my heart."

My heart.

The horse shifted behind Lazaro, bumping his shoulder, moving him forward. Zoe felt the wave of heat, and the shimmer of energy as he moved near her. She could feel him everywhere and he wasn't even touching her. His strength was a tangible thing, his chemistry so powerful that blood surged to her cheeks and her belly clenched in helpless knots of feeling.

Of wanting. Of desire.

He was watching her, his lips curving ever so slightly. "Is there anything else you want to know?"

Just how to get out of here, she answered silently, panicked all over again. No man had ever affected her like this.

They rode beneath the thicket of birch, oak and acacia trees protecting the house and grounds, reached open grasslands, and loosened the reins so the horses could run.

Lazaro rode hard, fast, and Zoe had to lean forward in the saddle, knees gripped tight, just to keep up with him. She found it frightening riding so fast. Daisy always liked to fly when riding but Zoe was the careful one, the cautious. She hated losing control, feared falling, getting hurt. Feared lots of things, when she thought about it.

The wind blew her hair free and stung her eyes. She blinked hard and clung harder with her knees. *You don't have to do this. You don't have to go this fast.*

But she didn't stop, and she didn't call out to him. She'd show him she could keep up. She'd show him she was tough.

They rode up a hill, down the hill, and up another slope, this one steeper than the last. The grass was taller, coarser, and now and then her horse would stumble on half-buried rocks and Zoe would feel her heart leap to her throat.

She chased Lazaro along the top of the hill, boots deep in the stirrup, sun shining warmly above. Looking down through the bright glaze of sunlight she realized they were riding along the edge of a ravine. Trying not to give in to fear, she peered over, and the drop went way, way down. Far below she caught a glimpse of white water swirling. A river. And rocks. Lots of them.

My God, one stumble and they'd go all the way over.

Zoe steered her mare from the edge, and caught the look Lazaro shot her way.

"Nervous?" he asked, reining in his horse and waiting for her.

"No," she lied, panting a little. To hide her trembling she leaned over and gave her horse an encouraging pat.

"Good. Because we're going to ride down and have lunch on the river."

Zoe wanted to throw up. "Ride down?"

"To the river." He gestured toward the steep cliff. "You all right with that?"

Say no, say no, say no. "Sure," she choked, trying to sound nonchalant even as her heart pounded at an appalling speed.

His stallion did a little two-step, drifting sideways, eager to be moving again. "Let's do it."

Just don't look down, she told herself as she steered her horse toward the steep slope and deep ravine.

Jaw clamped tight, feet pressed deep in stirrups, Zoe's heart lurched with every stumble and slip as the horse scrambled down the mountain. The horse's hooves thudded against rocks and dust poofed in fine brown clouds as dirt clouds skidded, bounced and fell to the gully below.

Her heart was doing the same free fall and her stomach heaved up, once, twice, with violent measure.

Awful, awful. I hate this. I'll never do this again. Fear screamed through her, razor-hot and razor-fast. This was not her idea of riding. She liked dressage. She liked the ring. She loved jumping pretty white fences. Making her horse high-step. All the elegant, refined activity that earned her blue ribbons in competition but not this…not wild, abandoned dives down steep Argentine mountains.

She'd broken a sweat by the time they reached the river. Her hands shook so badly she gave up all pretense of even holding the reins.

Zoe drew her right leg over the horse and slid nervelessly out of the saddle. Her legs buckled and nearly gave way as she hit the ground.

"*¡Por Dios!* That was amazing." Lazaro's husky laugh reached her where she stood leaning weakly against the mare's warm expanded belly. That was the worst ride of her entire life. Amazing was not the right word by any stretch of the imagination.

She heard him jump from the saddle, his boots hitting the earth with a soft thud. "Hungry?" he asked.

Zoe staggered a step to the rocky outcropping. Her legs gave out. Her bottom slammed down on the warm granite. She was shaking uncontrollably and couldn't even clasp her knees. *"No."*

She'd never been so scared. She'd been certain

she'd fall, crash, burn. She'd been afraid of pain. Afraid of dying. Afraid of everything.

She was perspiring. Her skin felt cold and clammy. "Why did we come down here?"

"For the fun of it."

CHAPTER FOUR

ZOE shook her head, gasping. "That wasn't fun, that was crazy!"

But Lazaro wasn't offended. He laughed. He seemed *pleased.*

His boots crunched dirt and rock as he walked toward her, his shadow looming large and dark. He held out the plastic bottle. "Water."

She was so angry with him she couldn't answer and she didn't take the bottle.

He nudged her, stepping between her bent legs to tap one of her knees with his own. "Come on, drink."

She moved her legs to break contact with him. Her knee felt hot from his touch and her skin sensitive, almost bruised. But she didn't have the energy to argue with him and knew that even if she did nothing would be accomplished by it.

Zoe took the water bottle and gulped a mouthful. The water tasted cool and it did refresh her, but she was still angry. Very angry.

He stepped aside, taking a seat next to her on the boulder. "You're really mad, aren't you?"

"Yes."

"You didn't enjoy the ride down?"

"Hated it."

"Why?"

"It was terrifying."

56

"But exciting."

"I didn't find it exciting, I was too worried about sticking in the saddle."

"Then you shouldn't worry so much. You should trust yourself more. You're an excellent horsewoman. One of the best I've seen."

She didn't feel like it. She didn't feel like the best of anything. "I don't need to be flattered."

"It's not flattery, it's the truth. I was watching you closely, Zoe, making sure you were okay, and you were. You handled your horse beautifully. She's not an easy horse. She's one of my most spirited and yet you never lost control, not even for a moment."

His words hummed inside of her, and the sun grazed the top of her head, hot and bright, but it was nothing like the warmth she felt deep inside of her, warmth stirred to life by that one brief brush against her knee, the press of his jeans-clad leg to her own.

She shouldn't respond to such a little touch but she did. She shouldn't listen to the hum of his voice and his words in her head. Instead she was feeling everything, listening to everything, wanting everything.

It was like fire beneath her skin. Fire and lava, smoke and ash. She wanted more from him and she knew that more would burn her alive, scorch her with the intensity.

"Daisy was always the better rider," Zoe said faintly. "Daisy is the definition of tough."

"Until now."

Her brow creased. How right he was. She'd never thought of it that way, but yes, Daisy had always been tough until the miscarriages.

Lazaro suddenly lifted her left hand to inspect the ring on her finger. "So tell me about the lucky guy."

She shifted uncomfortably. She really wasn't engaged, had only worn the ring after Carter insisted she keep it while she consider his proposal. She'd turned him down but he hadn't accepted the rejection. He'd begged her to take some time and think about his marriage offer while she visited her sister in Argentina. Zoe hadn't known what to do with the ring, either, and in the end had slipped it on her finger so she wouldn't lose it. "Carter," she said faintly.

"Who?"

"Carter. Carter Scott."

"Nice guy, I bet."

"Just great." She wasn't about to tell Lazaro that she had no intention of marrying Carter, and that she'd agreed to consider Carter's proposal only because she hadn't wanted to hurt his feelings. Carter and her father had been friends for years and after Daisy moved to Argentina, Carter had begun to befriend her, as well, taking her out for dinner, inviting her to parties and other Lexington society events.

"You must love him a great deal," Lazaro persisted.

She tugged her hand free. "He's a gentleman."

"Unlike me."

"Definitely unlike you."

Lazaro picked up a twig and turned the broken twig in his hands, examining the dove-gray bark, the tiny branches, the two small dried leaves still clinging to the branches. "He wants children?"

She tried not to squirm, unable to imagine making

love to Carter, a man close to her father's age. "He's…family oriented."

"I'd love to meet him."

"Sure." She balled her hands in her lap. "Once you're out of prison, give me a call. We'll see what we can arrange."

Lazaro threw back his head and almost roared with laughter. "Prison?"

"That's where you'll be going for kidnapping."

"Kidnapping?" he repeated, still chuckling.

"Yes, *kidnapping*." She shot him a cutting glance. "Or is there something else you expect to go to prison for?"

He appeared to think it over before shrugging. "No, taking you is probably the worst I've done…so far."

So far. And he didn't even sound repentant. She shot him another scathing side glance and froze.

Suddenly she couldn't tear her gaze from his face. How could anyone with such a hard heart be so beautiful?

With his outrageously long eyelashes, and the sunlight pouring down on his head, she could see the flecks of silver and pewter in his irises, silver and pewter against smoke. Like the Kentucky mist rising from the meadows, or the rich patina on a piece of heirloom sterling.

How could she find him so attractive? How could she feel this kind of desire? What kind of person was she to want a man without morals, scruples, a shred of decency?

Thank God for her fake engagement. If it weren't

for the fact that she had to pretend to care about Carter, she might do something silly...might throw herself at Lazaro and beg for the pleasure and the passion she was sure she'd find in his bed.

Zoe turned her head away, looked toward the splashing river with the swirls of white foam and jagged points of rock. The sun reflected off the water in bright sheets of light and seemed to illuminate even her heart.

If she didn't escape Lazaro soon, she'd do something stupid.

She'd beg Lazaro to touch her, make love to her.

Lazaro tossed down the twig. ''We should start back. We've got a long ride home.''

They rode along the riverbank, crossing the stream to travel up a grassy hill dotted with oaks and birch trees. The terrain leveled out, turning into more gold grasslands beneath an endless blue sky.

Zoe squinted. A building appeared in the distance. The building became a cluster of buildings. Buildings, fences, cows.

People.

Zoe's heart thudded. People who could help her. People who could call for help.

Swiftly she calculated the distance, measuring the time it'd take to reach them. Even riding hard, she might not be able to outride Lazaro, but perhaps she could attract their attention.

If she did it, she'd have to act quickly. No mistakes. No second thoughts. No exceptions. Could she do it? Hell, yes.

Zoe leaned forward in the saddle, pressed her knees

tight to the mare, and with a tug on the rein steered the horse to a sharp left.

Lazaro's voice rang out. "Wrong way."

She ignored him. Didn't even look back. The wind hummed in her ears and stung her eyes. She blinked and crouched low, holding on even tighter as she focused on her goal. The people in the distance, the people who would help her, the people—

"Zoe!"

His voice crackled with authority. He expected her to stop. He was demanding she stop. Commanding her to stop.

But she wouldn't. She rode on, hair blowing wildly, fingers bloodless around the leather reins.

She heard him riding on her, heard him closing the distance, his stallion's hooves pounding as though the cavalry pursued her.

Just another minute, she told herself, hang on, keep riding. An ear-splitting whistle shattered the air and suddenly the mare drew up short, breaking her stride.

Lazaro whistled a second time and the mare's forelegs left the ground and the horse reared back.

Zoe wasn't prepared for her horse to buck and couldn't keep her feet planted in the stirrups. She knew she was going to get thrown but didn't have time to break her fall. Within seconds she was sailing head over heels, and slammed hard to the ground.

The impact knocked her silly.

For a moment she couldn't move, much less think. She dragged in a breath and staggered to her feet. Dazed and yet unwilling to give up, she began limping toward the house in the distance.

"Zoe, stop."

He could go to hell. She wasn't going to stop for anything.

"Zoe, I'm warning you."

Tears smarted her eyes and she limped on, determined to reach help.

Whomph!

Zoe felt herself slam down a second time, this time leveled by Lazaro's shoulder.

She felt the weight of him on her, felt the hard prickle of the grass beneath her, felt the air sail out of her even as pain washed through her.

He'd tackled her. Like a football, or a calf being roped at a rodeo. He'd tackled her.

In a dim part of her brain she registered that a lady should never be treated this way.

But he didn't think of her as a lady.

She felt his warm breath tickle the back of her neck, heard his muttered oath as he shifted his weight off her and brushed the tangled blond hair from her cheek. "Where does it hurt?" he asked, voice raspy.

She was still lying facedown in the ground where she was eating dirt and clumps of grass, and she pushed herself up on an elbow. "Go to hell!"

"I didn't want to do that."

"Don't talk to me."

"I would never want to hurt you."

She dragged herself to her knees and brushed the dirt from her hands, and then used her forearm to wipe her mouth and face. "Stay away from me."

"I'm not going to let you run away."

"No, you made that pretty clear," she grunted, peeling a stalk of grass from her forearm.

"Promise me you won't try that again."

"I'm not going to promise anything of the sort! You've kidnapped me. This isn't a vacation."

He wiped at the dirt powdering his hair and brow. "At least we agree on that."

"Send me back to Buenos Aires. *Please.*"

"Not an option."

"When will it be an option?"

"When the takeover goes public."

She stared at him for a long moment, scrambling to make sense of this last bit of information, and then understanding the big picture better. "You're going after Dante's company."

He stood up. "It's been the goal."

"All these years."

"All these years," he agreed, whistling for his horse.

She stared at him in shock. "How did I get mixed up with the takeover?"

"Timing."

"I don't get it."

"You were never part of the plan. But when Dante approached me I couldn't say no."

Fury swept through her. "Why not?"

He shrugged, reached for his stallion's bridle. "It was too great of an opportunity. I could seize Dante's company even as I framed him with kidnapping. Revenge can't get much sweeter."

She walked away from him, staggering as though drunk. Her head spun. Her stomach thumped. She thought she was going to be sick. "Where's my horse?"

"Gone." Lazaro pointed to the horizon. "Back to my *estancia,* I imagine."

Gritty tears stung the backs of her eyes. She felt ridiculously helpless and painfully reliant on him. This was a disaster on top of disasters.

Sliding one foot in the stirrup, Lazaro swung the other leg over the saddle then leaned down and extended her a hand. "*Por favor,* climb up."

"No, thank you."

"I'm not going to let you run away."

"I'll walk back."

"You'll still try to run away."

"I'm not that stupid. You've knocked me to the ground twice. Do you honestly think I want to do that a third time?"

He had the gall to laugh and his soft laughter goaded her, made her see red.

"I don't know, *corazón,* but somehow I don't think you've given up on running away."

"Go away!"

"Can't do that, *corazón*—"

"I'm not your *corazón!*"

"Yes, you are. Now give me your hand."

He rode up beside her and she glared at him, hating the way the sunshine played his features perfectly, his nose bent, crooked, but still Roman above his sensual lips. No wonder it had been broken so many times. He had to have thousands of enemies.

"Give me your hand," he said softly.

"No way."

"Then we'll do it my way."

Lazaro leaned over, twisted a finger in her belt loop and hauled her onto his lap.

Zoe dropped into the saddle. Her bottom slammed against his hips, throwing her into shockingly intimate contact. She made a desperate wiggle to escape but he clamped an impossibly muscular arm around her waist and held her firm.

"Sit still," he muttered hoarsely, "or you'll knock us both off."

She gave a futile kick, missed his leg entirely. "Put me down!"

"It's not going to happen." His palm pressed flat to her stomach, fingers spread across her belly, creating tension and fire in every nerve. The sensation of his hand on her tummy, the firm insistent pressure against her pelvis, made her feel incredibly conscious of him, of her, of them together.

"Take your hands off me," she gritted from between clenched teeth. *"Please."*

She felt his chest rise and fall, his ribcage expanding as he drew a short, impatient breath. "I'm not about to let go, *señorita*. I'm tired of hunting you down like a jackrabbit—"

Her elbow found a home in his ribs and he grunted with pain. "If I'm a jackrabbit you're an ass!"

She suddenly felt his hand tug her ponytail, drawing her head back. "You must like to live dangerously," he said, his mouth brushing her ear. One of his hands slid the length of her throat to span the fragile bones in her jaw.

A shudder raced down her spine as she felt a surge

of awareness, a primitive knowledge that they were
so very different from each other. He was made differently, shaped bigger, harder, more powerfully. He
thought differently, too, and yet something about him,
something in him, made her feel strongly. Intensely.

Love, hate…what was the difference? The way she
felt now it was all so fierce, all so passionate, she
couldn't figure out what she wanted from him, and
whether she wanted his touch or wanted to be left
alone.

Could opposites really attract like this?

Zoe closed her eyes as his lips traveled across her
cheekbone and kissed the corner of her mouth. The
kiss sent sharp darts of sensation through her, made
her belly clench and her breath catch in her throat.

She felt his hips cradle hers, felt the firmness of his
hand against her waist. She could almost imagine him
with her, naked, could almost imagine the feel of his
skin and the press of his hard body against hers.

It would be both pleasure and pain.

It would be more erotic and more intense than anything she'd ever felt.

He kissed her lower lip and her mouth trembled
beneath his. She gripped the pommel on the saddle,
fought the desire to touch his leg, cover his thigh with
her hand. She wanted to touch him, wanted to draw
closer to him but couldn't. Despite her desire, she
couldn't let this happen, couldn't give in to the craving for contact, for heat, for skin.

He was dangerous. He was amoral. He'd destroy
her if she wasn't careful.

''Stop,'' she whispered faintly against his mouth,

hoping he wouldn't hear her, and yet needing him to have more control than she did, more discipline than she felt.

He lifted his head. He looked down at her, his light eyes shadowed. ''Of course. I can be as much of a gentleman as your Carter.''

The ride back seemed to last forever. Every step the horse took jostled her against him, his thighs rubbing hers, his body touching hers, his heat scalding her. Every jostle and touch fueled her imagination. By the time they reached the stable she was tense and wound tight from head to toe. Nerve endings she didn't even know existed tingled, tormenting her with sensation that she didn't want or need.

Reaching the stable, she swung a leg over the saddle and scrambled to the ground, too hot and raw to be touched a second longer.

Lazaro didn't say anything as she fled the stable, but then, he didn't have to, she thought with a shudder. He knew perfectly well the effect he had on her and they both knew it was only a matter of time now before she cracked, and her defenses fell.

Lazaro leaned on the pommel and watched Zoe escape the stable. She wasn't running, but came damn close.

She didn't like him, but she wanted him.

He had a suspicion she didn't want Carter Scott, but felt safe marrying him. Dante was right about one thing. Carter Scott didn't deserve Zoe. At fifty-three, Carter was over twice her age and notoriously lecherous.

Lazaro had looked into Carter Scott, in fact, he

wasn't sure he would have agreed to Dante's scheme if Carter had been a decent man, but Carter wasn't decent. Carter had a weakness for young blondes in distress. He'd proposed to Daisy three years ago, practically knuckling her into marrying him to save the family farm, and now with Daisy out of the picture, he was doing the same to Zoe.

Lazaro's gut tightened. He'd be damned if he let Carter have her. The American didn't have a moral bone in his body.

Suddenly he stopped himself, and grimaced, mouth contorting. Judging Carter Scott felt a little like the pot calling the kettle black. It wasn't his place.

But that was the problem, he thought, unsaddling his stallion. He didn't know his place. Literally.

In thirty years of searching, in thirty years of struggling, he'd never found a place to call home.

He'd never found the place he belonged.

CHAPTER FIVE

ZOE headed for the pool after the ride hoping a swim would work the kink out of her knotted muscles. The twenty laps did help with her knotted muscles but it didn't do much for her tension, or for her craving for Lazaro's skin.

How could she want anyone so much? How could she physically want someone like this?

She'd had a couple of boyfriends, nothing serious, and while they'd made out, they'd never made love. She loved to kiss but she hadn't felt sufficient interest to go all the way…until now.

Somehow she knew she'd find what she wanted with Lazaro, she knew he understood the tension within her, knew he responded with passion.

Already his brief kisses turned her inside out, made her body tremble and ache, but the intensity of her desire frightened her, and more than just a little. Lazaro was the wrong man to want, the wrong man to need. He might represent passion but he also represented chaos. And destruction.

Disgusted with herself, Zoe climbed from the pool, toweled off and was just about to take a seat on one of the lounge chairs when she heard the back door to the house open and close.

Her heart jumped as she spotted Lazaro making his way toward the pool. He was wearing only a pair of black swim trunks and his very broad shoulders emphasized the narrow width of his waist and the length of his muscular legs.

He was all man, she thought, panicking all over again, and she grabbed for her things, dumping the suntan lotion and sunglasses into her straw bag and shoving her feet into flip-flops.

"Nice swim?" he asked as she rushed past.

She couldn't even meet his gaze. "Great, thank you," she said, hurrying on toward the house.

Zoe reached the door, turned the knob, and realized with a stab of horror that her left hand was bare. The engagement ring was missing. That huge, expensive rock was gone.

No! She couldn't lose it, she had to give it back to Carter!

Zoe returned to the pool just in time to see a flash of bronze skin and black swim trunks break the surface of the water. She froze at the gate and watched him swim the length of the pool underwater, rising only once he'd reached the other side.

Lazaro pushed up and out of the water, taking a seat on the pool's tiled edge. Water streamed from his hair, his bronzed skin, the sinewy planes of his body.

With one hand he raked his wet hair back, scraping the glistening ebony waves from his brow. His skin gleamed all over, minute water droplets clinging to his chest.

His head lifted and he caught sight of her standing there, staring at him, absolutely transfixed. He leaned back on his arms, accenting the bulge of his bicep and thickness of the tricep. "Need something?" he drawled.

"Yes," she stammered, sick at heart. "I've lost my ring. The engagement ring."

"The ring from Carter?"

"Yes." Heart racing, she watched as he rose from the side of the pool and walk toward the lounge chairs. "It was his mother's ring. It's an old family heirloom."

He lifted his towel and rubbed it over his chest, down his flat belly and across his wet swim trunks. She couldn't tear her gaze away, fascinated by the ripple of muscle and display of strength.

Lazaro glanced at her and one of his black eyebrows lifted. "*Corazón,* in case you were wondering, I don't have the ring on me."

Mortified, she felt another tide of color surge to her cheeks. She forced herself to move, walking past him to the lounge chair where she'd placed her things earlier. She knelt down, skimmed her hands over the lounge chair cushion, under the cushion and then beneath the chair itself.

"Perhaps you lost it on the ride," Lazaro said, briskly drying his hair before using his fingers to rake the wet crisp hair smooth.

She stood up, shook her head, both frustrated and worried. "I'm pretty sure I had it when I returned to the house." She circled the lounge chair, walked to the edge of the pool, gazed down at the pool bottom. "I shouldn't have worn it. I shouldn't have brought it on this trip. I'll never be able to pay him back."

"I'm sure he won't expect you to pay him back."

"But I'll have to. The diamond was four carats. It's worth a fortune."

"Is that what he told you?"

She stiffened and slowly faced him. "Yes, and why shouldn't he?"

"Because it's not a real diamond."

"What?"

"The stone's fake." He shrugged, immense shoulders shifting as he walked toward her. "It's not even a good imitation."

Zoe staggered back a step, aghast. How dare he! What a revolting thing to say! Just who did he think he was?

Indignant tears burned her eyes and she reached into her straw bag for her sunglasses, but her movements were jerky and instead of landing neatly on her nose the glasses tumbled to the ground.

Lazaro bent over and retrieved the tortoiseshell glasses and, standing, gently placed the frame on the bridge of her nose.

His fingers grazed her ears and he adjusted the bridge piece higher. "Tell me about Carter. Tell me why you love him."

Lazaro's voice wrapped around her heart and she quivered on the inside, hunger, awareness, desire coiling so tight that she felt almost brittle with the intensity of the need. She looked at him through the dark-tinted shades, her pulse racing hard and fast.

How could she keep up this charade? How could she pretend to love Carter when all she wanted was to touch Lazaro, to be in his arms, to feel his mouth against hers? "He's a family friend," she answered faintly. "I've known him forever."

"And that's enough for you?"

"He's good to Dad. He helps with him… sometimes."

Lazaro's brow furrowed, eyes narrowing. "This is your idea of love?"

"I—"

"You what?"

Her lips parted but she couldn't speak. She felt dizzy, light-headed.

His gaze dropped to her mouth and lingered there, as though he could remember the feel of her lips and taste of her mouth.

If only he'd kiss her again…if only he'd touch her now…but he didn't. He just stood there watching, waiting, making her face feel hot, her cheekbones sensitive. She should walk away right now, put some distance between them, but her legs wouldn't move. "Carter's not like that," she defended huskily.

Lazaro pounced. "Like what?"

"Like…bad…evil. He's not that way."

"Maybe he's not evil, but he's not a good person, and he's not a good choice for you."

Zoe flinched at his tone. His voice had cooled and hardened so that the words came out like hail stones, icy, sharp, painful. "How can you say that? You don't even know him."

"I know enough. I know that Carter and I are both con artists. We've made careers out of manipulating the system. I manipulate the Galváns. Carter manipulates pretty young blondes."

"But if that's all—"

Lazaro didn't get it, didn't understand how Zoe could keep defending Carter unless she really and truly loved him.

"It's not all," he interrupted shortly, his temper barely leashed, anger making him see red. "Your Carter Scott is worse than a petty criminal. He's been under investigation for tax evasion, forgery, insurance fraud, including two cases of suspected arson." *Including the fire at your farm three and a half years ago.*

But Zoe didn't believe him, he could see it in the defiant tilt of her chin and the twist of her lips.

"Just because you're amoral, Lazaro, doesn't make every other man amoral, too."

He shook his head, words failing him. He didn't know how to explain to her the circumstances that had brought them together like this. He didn't know where to even begin describing his past, and his mother's disgrace. "I may not be a virtuous man but I'd never take advantage of a woman."

"No, then what do you call holding me here against my will?" Her voice quivered with rage. "I'm your hostage. You're keeping me here, prisoner. Isn't this taking advantage of me? Isn't this denying me my rights?"

He hated the tears in her eyes, hated the loathing on her lovely face. "Yes," he said at last, his voice pitched low, and rough.

She lifted a finger, pointed it at his chest. "Then don't you talk to me about Carter and don't you lecture me about my choices because you are lower than low, you are absolutely completely despicable.''

In his suite of rooms, at his desk in the corner office, Lazaro stared at the pages spitting out of his fax machine.

The takeover had begun. The board members had been notified, the shareholders contacted, the offer made. Now it was a matter of time and patience. And nerves of steel. Because Lazaro could imagine what Dante was going through right now, he could imagine his half brother's shock, anger, and sense of betrayal.

Dante had believed in him.

But Dante had never known him.

The fax machine continued to churn, printing page after page of legal documents. Offer of intent to buy. Price per share. Acquisition of stock.

Dante must be reeling.

The door to his office squeaked open. Zoe stood there in the doorway, a sundress pulled over her pink and white floral bikini.

Her long golden hair had been scraped back and twisted into a severe knot at the back of her head. She wore no makeup and her eyes were enormous, dark lavender shadows in her pale face. ''I want proof,'' she said curtly. ''Give me proof that Dante was behind this or let me go. Now.''

Lazaro didn't look well, she thought, as she stood in the doorway watching him read through the reams of pages spilling from the fax machine. His color was off, his complexion a mottled gray, and deep lines formed at his eyes and mouth, aging him considerably.

He dropped the papers he'd been holding onto his desk. "Proof?"

"Yes. You must have some documentation somewhere. Something in writing that would incriminate Dante. That's how you'd do it, too. You'd get it in writing so you could torture him later."

She heard herself spit the words at him and each word hurt her and she didn't know why. She was wanting to wound him and yet this only made her ache, her heart mashed to nothing by a situation bigger than any of them.

In her room, she realized she didn't know what to believe anymore. She didn't know who to trust.

Lazaro had done this to her. He'd taken her world and turned it inside out.

How had he done it? How had he knocked her so completely off balance?

Maybe it was because he spoke to her simply, and he spoke directly. He didn't mince words. He didn't try to protect her feelings while Daisy and Dante, her father and even Carter were always trying to shield her from things, and make decisions for her. Her family meant well but it was, she knew now, a disservice.

But Lazaro didn't try to protect her. He'd told her the facts, or his version of the facts, and somehow what he said made sense. She didn't agree with him but she appreciated his honesty. If it was honesty.

Which was why she was here, demanding proof. She didn't know truth from the lies anymore, and refused to let him tie her insides up in knots any longer.

She wanted facts, the cut-and-dried details, and she'd decide for herself what was right, and what was true.

"I know you have paperwork," she added stiffly, her stomach churning, her legs weighted with lead. "I'd like to see whatever it is you have, please."

Lazaro handed her the file and he watched her open the folder and begin to read. She was right, he thought grimly, she knew him well enough to know he'd document everything regarding Zoe's situation, he'd make sure he was covered in case this became a legal situation.

He wouldn't go down without implicating Dante. He wouldn't take the fall without destroying Dante's name and reputation.

Zoe's hands shook as she leafed through the paperwork. He saw her swallow, her pale throat tightening, knotting as she fought for control over her emotions.

The paperwork he'd saved would upset her. There were e-mails from Dante and photos of her at the Collingsworth farm. He saw her study a copy of her passport, examine a printout of her airline itinerary and a transfer of funds between bank accounts.

She closed the folder and slid it across his desk. "He paid you to do this."

Lazaro heard the wobble in her voice. "The funds are actually for you, in case you needed cash while here."

Zoe made a hoarse sound. "Why would I need cash? I'm your guest here. Everything has been so thoughtfully provided for me."

"He didn't mean to hurt you, Zoe."

"Don't defend him. You're his enemy!"

His chest felt tight. "But you're hurt, this hurts, I can see it in your face—"

"Which should make you happy," she interrupted with a brittle laugh. "This is exactly what you wanted, so celebrate."

But he wasn't feeling celebratory. He felt sick inside. Felt awful. Evil. Not like himself at all. "I can't celebrate your unhappiness, Zoe. I care too much about you."

She laughed again and then the laugh turned to a sob and her eyes were filling with tears. "Don't say you care about me, that's the worst insult of all. You don't care about me. You don't care about anyone. You live only for yourself."

"There's so much you don't know."

"I don't think so." Her gaze met his and held. "I think that's the lie you tell yourself, but I think the truth is actually quite simple. You want others to hurt because you hurt. So pour yourself a drink and enjoy your success. You're good. You're good at being cruel. You're really good at what you do."

She walked out of his office, leaving his door open. He stared at the open door, listened to her footsteps echo and then disappear and felt the silence swallow him whole.

This was supposed to have played out differently. He thought he was so smart, thought he knew what he was doing taking Zoe, turning her against Dante, but it wasn't working out the way he'd imagined.

It was one thing to exact revenge on his half

brother. It was another to involve an innocent young woman.

His father was the one who hurt innocent girls, not him. Never him. He'd vowed to protect innocence and yet here he was, holding Zoe hostage, keeping her here against her will.

What kind of man did that to a woman?

A man like his father. But he wasn't his father. He was nothing like his father.

Or was he?

In her yellow bedroom with the dark-stained beams, Zoe dragged her black suitcase from the closet and tossed it on her bed. She blinked away stupid tears as she unzipped the suitcase and flipped the top open.

So it was all true. What Lazaro had said was true. Dante had orchestrated the entire abduction. He'd even deposited money into Lazaro's account.

How could Dante do this to her? What kind of person was he?

Tears blinded her vision and she furiously wiped them away. It was dumb to cry. Crying wouldn't change anything. The only way things would change is if she left, which was exactly what she was going to do.

Blinking, she marched on the dresser and opened the drawers, scooping up shirts and shorts and knit skirts.

"*Corazón,* where do you think you're going?"

Lazaro's voice came from the doorway, his tone surprisingly gentle.

She blinked back scalding tears. "Away."

"Now? At nine o'clock at night?"

Thank God he wasn't lampooning her. He could, she knew, make fun of her. They both knew there was nowhere for her to go, that if she left now she'd be walking in the dark in the middle of nowhere, but he didn't say any of that and she just kept packing.

She shook her head, and returned to the dresser, gathering her panties and bras and dumping them in the suitcase. "I have to go. I can't stay here anymore. I can't be near you anymore."

"Okay."

Okay? She stilled, her hands resting on the edges of her suitcase, and looked up at him. "You agree?"

"Yes."

"So you'll let me go, you'll get your helicopter to come for me?"

"Yes, tomorrow morning. First thing. I promise."

"Why not now?"

"It's late. It was a big day for my business today and my pilot had a long day. He needs his rest, but I'll send for him in the morning."

"How do I know I can believe you?"

"Have I lied to you yet?"

She stared at him for a long, hard minute. She saw him for what he was, and wanted to hate him, but she couldn't. She felt strong things for him, intense things, but hate wasn't one of them.

She moved to her closet, crouched down and grabbed pairs of shoes, drawing them into a pile. And then there, on the bottom of the closet, she saw a glint of white fire against gold.

The ring.

Carter's mother's ring.

Zoe picked up the ring, slid it on her finger and stood. "I found it," she said, turning around and facing Dante. "It was here. On the floor of the closet."

Lazaro leaned against her door frame. "I'm glad you found it."

She frowned. "Why? You think it's fake."

"But you were worried. I don't want you to worry anymore. I want you to be happy. You deserve to be happy."

Suddenly she wished she hadn't slipped the ring onto her finger. She didn't want it there. Didn't like it there. "I don't think Carter's bad," she said softly, balling her fingers into a fist, "but I don't really know him very well and—" she drew a breath, looked up at Lazaro "—and I don't love him, I've never been in love with him. We're not even really engaged."

Lazaro straightened. "What?"

She shook her head, chewed her lower lip, her expression rueful. "You and Dante are both so clever and yet you're so wrong on this one. I was never engaged to Carter, I never promised to marry him. He asked me but I didn't say yes."

CHAPTER SIX

LAZARO moved from the doorway toward her bed. He touched her suitcase. "I don't understand. You have the ring, you've been wearing it the whole time you were here."

Zoe would have laughed if she had the energy. Lazaro's expression was priceless. He looked absolutely stunned. "He insisted I keep it while I consider his proposal, and I was afraid I'd lose it so I wore it." She made a face. "Only I almost lost it wearing it so I don't know how smart that was."

"You don't love Carter."

"No."

"You never even considered marrying him?"

She puzzled over the question, felt the press of the diamond against her skin. "I'm sure I considered it. I'd be a fool not to consider it. I don't have that many options. I should try to keep some open."

It was true. Since Daisy had moved to Argentina, Zoe had been so alone, and so much on her own. She felt no safety or security, no support, either. Daisy had her new life with Dante and Zoe had been left behind to manage their father's care. Zoe didn't mind the responsibility, but it was lonely. In fact, it was downright overwhelming at times.

He sat down on the bed, next to the suitcase. "But Dante really believes you're engaged to Carter. He said he'd talked to Carter, that Carter had phoned him with the news.''

Zoe reached for her cowboy boots and held them against her chest. ''Then Dante should have talked to me. I could have set him straight, but why talk to me? I'm just Daisy's kid sister and too silly to make a good decision on my own.''

''I don't think that's what Dante meant—''

''Stop defending him!'' She tossed the boots into the suitcase so hard they nearly bounced back out. ''You're not on the same side. You can't see his point of view, you can't agree with him and you can't try to patch things up, either.''

She retreated to the bathroom, gathered her bottles of shampoo, conditioner and bath gel and carried them back to her suitcase. ''Are you really going to let me leave here tomorrow?''

''Yes.''

She dropped the bottles into the suitcase next to the boots, and leaned on the suitcase. ''Good. Because I want to go home.'' She looked up at him, her eyes meeting his silver gaze. ''You'll take me to the airport, get me on a plane?''

''What about Daisy?''

She felt her eyes burn. ''What about Daisy?''

''You came to see her.''

Her fragile control was beginning to crack. Her hands shook as she pressed the bunched-up clothes flat. ''I do want to see her but I don't want to see Dante and there's no way I can see her without him.''

''True,'' he agreed.

She marched away from the suitcase, arms crossed

over her chest. She felt angry and disorganized and utterly beside herself. "How could Dante of all people do this?"

Lazaro's voice followed her. "People make mistakes. Dante made a mistake."

She spun to face him. "I can't believe you keep feeling the need to take his side. You're supposed to be the bad guy. Act like the bad guy, for heaven's sake!"

He rose from the bed, moved toward her. "And what would the bad guy do right now?"

"Smile. Laugh. Savor my torment."

The atmosphere in the bedroom suddenly felt charged and the tension reverberated through Zoe.

Lazaro reached out to smooth a long tangle of hair from her cheek. "I can't savor anything. I'm sorry. I'm sorry I've done this to you."

Her heart squeezed tight within her. "Don't apologize to me. I can't stand the sympathy. It's not like you."

Her rough protest drew a wry smile to his lips. "No, it's not like me. I'm not hero material, am I?"

She couldn't answer him, couldn't speak, not because she was angry with him but because she didn't understand how she could want him now, at a time like this. It didn't make sense to her, this intense desire.

He tucked another tendril behind her ear and the brush of his fingertips against her skin sent darts of feeling from her nipples to her belly and beyond.

She felt him everywhere, felt him in her skin, her muscles, her blood, her bones. He'd only touched her cheek but she felt his warmth and his strength. "I want you," she breathed, her voice strangled. "I need you."

His hands circled her upper arms, fingers firm against her skin. He tried to push her away but she didn't move. His gaze searched hers and she saw his inner struggle, his unwillingness to let this happen. He gave his head a small brief shake. "I can't do this, Zoe."

"Why not? You've done everything else."

"I'd just be taking advantage of you."

"As if that's stopped you before."

"This is different. Sex is different."

She stepped toward him, closing the distance between them. "But this isn't about sex," she whispered. "It's about wanting to be with you, wanting to know you—"

"But you do know me, and we both know what I am." His hands slid down the length of her arms, capturing her wrists. Her pulse leaped at the touch. She felt eagerness, excitement, desire, but absolutely no fear.

"I don't think it's that simple," she answered, her breath catching in her throat. For days she'd wanted to be held by him, touched by him, and it was all she could do not to beg for that which she wanted. "I don't think you're that simple. Yes, there are things about you I don't understand, but there are things about you I do."

He tilted her chin up, stared down into her eyes. "You make me afraid."

It was getting very hard to think clearly, very hard

to be rational. His touch, his warmth, his energy was wrapping her up, binding her to him. She didn't want words, she wanted sensation. Didn't need talk, needed passion.

"What is there to be afraid of?" she whispered.

"Loving you."

She stared at his mouth in fascination. Somehow, even though he was absolutely the wrong man for her, he made the most sense. "Don't be. I'm just Zoe."

"Yes, but I'm not what you need. I'm not an option. I can't be."

"Why not?"

"You know this one, *corazón*. We live in different worlds. Our futures have nothing in common."

He was saying the right thing, the smart thing, and yet she couldn't accept it. She stood up on tiptoe and gently touched her mouth to his. He stiffened and nearly drew back. She wrapped her hands around his neck, cupping his nape, and gently pulled his head back down to hers. "Kiss me."

"This will only make it harder—"

"I don't care." And she meant it. She'd never felt this kind of desire before, never felt so confident of herself as a woman before. She also knew that she and Lazaro had no future together, it would be impossible in the face of such animosity between their families, but for right now, this night, it felt right for them to be together.

Some things came only once in a lifetime, and suddenly she'd felt as though she'd waited her entire life for this. There were so many things she'd missed out on, so many people she'd already lost. Mom, Dad, Daisy. She'd didn't want Lazaro to be another regret.

Slipping her fingers into his crisp hair, she savored the thick silky texture.

She drew her lips across his, felt his breath caress her mouth, felt the contrast of skin and beard and shivered a little at the intensity of her own desire. She wanted him. Wanted to be taken by him, loved by him, possessed by him. ''Don't treat me like a little girl. I'm not a kid. I've been through more than most women twice my age and I know what I feel and I know what I need, and I need you. I need to be with you.''

His hands clasped her face, cradling her jaw in the span of his fingers. ''Have you ever made love before?''

''No. But you should be my first.''

Those words did something to him, melted the last of his icy reserve. She could see the protective wall crash down and his expression gentled, his silver gaze warming, his jaw easing.

The hunger he'd fought to contain was suddenly there on the surface and he wanted her, fiercely. She could feel his desire, feel his impatience and as color streaked beneath his cheekbones she placed her hands against his chest, touching the hard plane of muscle with her palms and then her fingertips. ''You're gorgeous,'' she whispered.

He felt amazing, too, and she wanted more. Lightly she slid her hands across the span of his chest following the curve of muscle and shape of ribs before discovering his small hard nipples beneath his linen shirt.

At the caress of her fingers he drew a sharp breath and Zoe looked up into his face, curious, eager, daring. She relished her role as seductress, wanted to know what he enjoyed and if it was similar to her pleasure.

Nails lightly raking, she stroked down his chest, beneath the rib to the taut flat abdomen. She could trace each of the ripples in his abdomen, feel the ridge and dip between muscle and the small indentation of his navel.

Fire surged in her veins, hunger and desire. Her hands hesitated for just a fraction at his belt before she unfastened the buckle and the button on the trousers.

"Have you undressed a man before?"

His question made her feel reckless. "No, but it's pretty much common sense, isn't it?"

He laughed softly, appreciatively, sending fresh trickles of feeling down her spine, trickles of fire in her belly. "Nothing feels common right now, *corazón.*"

His husky voice made her breathe deeply, and she felt a thrill of excitement tinged with shyness as she tugged his zipper down, then brushed his hipbones and the soft cotton of his briefs.

He was hard, straining against the cotton and she touched him uncertainly, not entirely sure what to do next and yet enjoying the part of the femme fatale.

Slipping her hand beneath the briefs she covered him with her hand, intrigued by the silky texture of his skin and the hard rigid length of him. He groaned, and grew even larger as she held him.

Suddenly Lazaro's head dipped and his lips covered hers. ''Zoe,'' he muttered thickly, hands stroking from her waist to her shoulders and then down again, making nerve endings dance the whole exquisite length.

It was a sweet relief when he tugged off her sundress. Stripped of everything but her bikini he carried her to the bed.

The mattress gave a little beneath her and Lazaro parted her thighs, moving between them. Hands on her ankles, he lightly circled the fragile bones and slowly caressed up, the shin, the curve of calf, the knee.

In just moments he'd melted the bones in her legs, set her trembling, her belly knotting in unabated need. She felt warm and hot inside and as he slid his hands up her outer thighs, her innermost muscles clenched.

He caressed back down her thighs, over the quadriceps to the knee and when his thumbs moved to the inside of her thighs she nearly jumped out of her skin.

His hands were a delicious torment, stroking lightly, teasingly, maddeningly up the inside of her thighs, fingers brushing at the sensitive hollows near the elastic of her bikini bottoms.

''Please,'' she gritted, reaching up to clasp his shoulders, the muscles bunched beneath her hands, his body hard, sleek, strong. She couldn't bear the bittersweet sensation of wanting another moment longer. She felt as though she'd been waiting forever for this moment. "Make love to me, Lazaro. Be part of me, now."

He unclasped her floral swimsuit top and drew it off, the sudden exposure drawing her nipples into aching buds. His warm mouth covered one bud, hot tongue laving the pebbled peak. She gasped, hands moving up his neck, against his scalp to grab fistfuls of silky hair. He felt hard and demanding, sexy and sinful, and she was beyond thinking. Her pelvis tipped, moving of its own accord, wanting to be closer, needing to be closer, her hips slowly grinding, arching, tilting against him.

"You are very much a woman," he mouthed against her breast, kissing his way up to find the line of collarbone, the hollow of her neck, the dip beneath her ear. His lips were firm, his tongue felt moist, his breath teased her sensitized skin.

Kissing her mouth, savoring the soft thrust of her lower lip, he stroked her from breast to belly, hand easing beneath her panties to cup her mound before discovering the warm moisture within.

Her breath was caught in his mouth, her gasp stolen by his lips. Nothing had ever felt like this before. Nothing had ever been so beautiful or so pleasurable.

When he stripped her of her bikini bottoms, tugging the flimsy scrap over her hips and curve of her derriere, she instinctively parted her legs, opening her knees for his body.

He made her feel like perfection and with a deep sigh, Zoe wrapped her arms around him and gave herself to him.

He entered her slowly, stopping once when she

tightened, feeling a sudden flicker of fear that he might be too big, too powerful.

Lazaro cupped her face in his hands, kissed her lower lip, sucked on it until she clasped his hands, hung on to him with all her might as her bones were dissolving, muscles melting, senses consuming.

She rose to meet his hips, draw him deeper, hold him completely inside.

"I don't want to hurt you," he whispered, holding back.

"You're not. It's lovely, you make me feel lovely."

He made a rough sound, and sank deeply into her body, filling her so that she could feel nothing but him and the blood pounding in her ears.

"You," he murmured, lips brushing her neck, her jaw, the corner of her lips, "are lovely."

He started to move, thrusting before nearly drawing out. She caught blindly at him, hands catching his ribs, fingers splayed against his warm chest. He moved back inside her and this time she moaned, feeling unbearable pleasure at the intensely erotic sensation of him in her, of them together.

The arch of her hips, the tilt of her pelvis, brought her fully into contact and created rivers of fire in every nerve of her body.

Feeling her respond, Lazaro thrust faster and she clung to him, each stroke arousing more sensation, stirring emotions and cravings she couldn't articulate. All she knew was that he couldn't stop and she couldn't let go.

Her heart pounded and her skin grew damp. The

thrusting became as much a torment as a pleasure. She felt something beyond the moment, felt something out there dancing beyond her, beckoning her forward. Zoe ground her hips, dug her nails into his arms, and pressed her teeth against his satin-covered shoulder.

Take me, take, take me, a silent voice inside her chanted as her muscles tensed, awareness building. She felt as though she'd never be able to hold on to him, never keep him with her, and never contain the building pressure. The desire was bigger than his body or hers, but something they'd created between them, something that had passed safety and reason, intellect and sensation. This was everything, and everything was consuming.

Her focus narrowed; silence filled her head. For a moment she saw nothing but a tiny light far away, but as Lazaro strained against her, his fingers weaving into her hair, holding her close, the tiny light flared up. Filled by him, pushed by him, she exploded, the tiny light becoming a great New Year's firework, white-silver spangles, sparkles, glitter. The intense buildup turned to hot, sweet, blinding bliss.

Bliss.

Oh heavens, it was better than the best, strong and yet seductively sweet. Still shuddering, she felt him arch, his body tensing, driving more deeply into her. Her orgasm pushed him over the edge and for an endless moment they were together in time and space.

At long last, trembling with near exhaustion, Zoe turned her face, kissed his shoulder and the warm spice of his skin. His heart thudded hard beneath her ear. His hair-roughened chest cradled her cheek. She felt like liquid on the inside and honey on the outside. Nothing, and no man, would ever rival this.

Nothing and no man would ever replace this.

Or him.

She didn't know how she knew, but she knew. Everything inside her had shifted, turned, become different and new. Stronger. More certain. Determined.

Lazaro Herrera might be Dante's enemy, but she needed him, might even love him.

Her breath caught in her throat and she opened her eyes to look up at him. He was braced on his elbows staring down at her, silver eyes focused, intense.

"Regrets?" he asked.

She didn't answer for a long moment, searching her heart, searching her conscience. Finally she shook her head. "No."

"Good." He dipped his head, covered her parted lips with his and kissed her deeply.

He was still beautifully warm, his skin damp, and she felt a floating calm. Rolling over, he drew her on top of him. Slowly, he stroked her hair, the dip in her spine, and the curve of her bottom.

"This is dangerous," he murmured.

"I shouldn't get pregnant. You took precautions."

"I'm not talking about that, I'm talking about you, about being with you. I could get very addicted to you, sweet Zoe, very addicted to this."

Her heart turned inside out. They were the right words if he'd been a different man, the right words if he could have been an option. How awful that they both knew that this was doomed from the start. "At least we had tonight," she answered huskily.

He kissed her again. "One night isn't enough."

It was the very thing she'd been thinking. Gritty tears stung the backs of her eyes. She reached out for him, her lips grazing his. "I don't want to think about tomorrow. I don't want tomorrow. Can't we pretend it won't come?"

He laughed but there was no warmth in his voice. Just pain. "I'm not very good at playing pretend."

"I guess you didn't have much of a childhood."

"Probably not enough," he agreed, lifting a strand of her hair, and caressing her flushed cheek. "I thought this would be hard," he added after a moment. "I didn't know it'd be this hard. You make me feel things again, Zoe. You make me want things I didn't think were possible."

She squeezed her eyes shut, pressed her face against his chest. She hurt on the inside, hurt when she thought of the intensity of her feelings and the impossibility of the situation.

He laughed again, curtly, angrily, as though he'd lost all patience with himself. "How am I going to let you go?"

Tears stung her eyes and she kissed his chest, before nestling closer. "Very, very carefully."

CHAPTER SEVEN

THEY'D fallen asleep after midnight, woken at four to make love yet once more. Zoe felt nerveless, her body deliciously relaxed. The lovemaking had completely and thoroughly exhausted her.

"Are you sure you don't want to go to Daisy's tomorrow?" Lazaro asked, his voice deep and rich in the dark, his fingertips lightly stroking her spine. "Your sister doesn't have to know about us. I won't tell and I'm quite sure Dante won't say anything."

"But once I arrive at Daisy's, I won't see you again, will I?"

"No."

She closed her eyes as his fingers trailed across her lower back. She wasn't ready to say goodbye, didn't know if she'd ever be ready to say goodbye, but knew she couldn't do it today. "Where are you going?"

"I've meetings in Buenos Aires."

"Oh." She couldn't hide her soft sigh of disappointment.

"I'd take you to the city with me, and we could spend another day or two together, but we're only avoiding the inevitable."

"Lots of things are inevitable," Zoe quipped, "including death." She suddenly thought of her father and his declining health, thought of the loneliness of the last two years since Daisy married and moved to Argentina. She didn't want to lose Lazaro, wondered if there wasn't some way that she could keep him in her life.

If he didn't persist with the takeover…

If he'd soften his stance against the Galváns…

"What's another day?" she murmured. "How will spending one more day together hurt?"

He was silent for a long moment before answering. "I have meetings late morning and a conference call after lunch, but I should be free before dinner. We could go out tomorrow night in the city. I could take you to my favorite restaurant."

It sounded wonderful. Dinner with Lazaro in the city. Dressing up, going out to his favorite restaurant. Yet he had meetings…business meetings…and she knew what those meant. "Your meetings tomorrow are part of the takeover?"

He caught her hand, carried it to his lips. "This isn't a choice, Zoe. This is something I have to do."

"Even if it's cruel?"

"I didn't start this."

"But you can finish it. You can be bigger than them, you can turn the other cheek—"

"No. I can't. I wish I could, but I can't. I'm not a gentle person. I am not a forgiving person and I can not forget the cruelty against my mother."

Zoe turned her face away, unable to bear hearing him talk this way. She couldn't reconcile herself to the harsh Lazaro, the Lazaro that lived for revenge. It wasn't the man she saw, and it wasn't the man she was falling in love with. "Then take me to Daisy's tomorrow," she choked. "Let's just get this over with."

Morning came and Zoe woke to the sound of a helicopter landing. Stirring she discovered Lazaro gone and for a moment she felt panic, thinking he'd left her here alone again. But then the bedroom door opened and he stood there, showered, shaved, dressed.

"Good morning," he said. "Luz has breakfast waiting."

He looked distant, his mouth tight, his expression shuttered. She tried to muster a smile but couldn't. "I'll shower quickly."

"Take your time. We'll leave when you're ready."

The helicopter ride to Buenos Aires was short in comparison to her memory of the trip out, and reaching the executive airport in Buenos Aires, they left the helicopter pad for the waiting limousine.

As they settled into the back of the car, Zoe's gaze fell on a crisp new newspaper lying on the seat. The huge black headlines were disproportionate to the rest of the headlines and included the word, Galván.

Zoe's heart leaped and fell, like a trout jumping in a stream. "What does that say?" she asked, pointing to the paper.

Lazaro looked at the newspaper lying on the leather seat. "'Rival Upstart Seizes Galván Wireless,'" he read tonelessly.

Lazaro was the rival upstart. He must have his own

company, must have other partners and investors. Dante would be reeling. "Read it all," she whispered.

"Why do you want to do this?"

"I want to know."

"You'll just get upset, and it won't change anything. The offer's made, the news is public, the wheels are already in motion."

The limousine had pulled out of the airport parking lot and was entering traffic. Sunlight glazed the limousine windows, dappling the interior of the car. Zoe gazed out the window. It was a gorgeous day, the sky an endless blue with just a few high, fat clouds scudding high above.

She turned to look at him, her heart mashed inside her chest. "So you might as well tell me just how bad it is."

He read the article, translating it for her, and by the end she felt physically sick. She covered her mouth, closed her eyes, wanting to be anywhere but trapped in the limousine with him.

Last night while they were making love he knew he was destroying Dante and Daisy's world...last night while holding her, loving her, he was annihilating another family's dreams.

"You knew about the takeover," he said flatly, breaking into her thoughts. "This isn't a complete surprise."

"I didn't realize it'd gone so far."

"It's been in the works for over a year."

"Poor Dante," she murmured, shaking her head.

"Poor Dante?" His voice blistered her. "What

about my mother? What about her? When the Galváns sent her away, she was just a schoolgirl, not even seventeen. What did she know about the world? How was she supposed to fend for herself, and a new baby? The Galváns had millions. Couldn't they at least send her away with a few dollars in her pocket?''

''It's been thirty-some years, Lazaro!''

''And that excuses what they did to her?''

''Not they, Lazaro, he, Tino, your father. But the whole family can't be held responsible!''

''Dante's mother was the one who insisted my mother be sent away. She was the one who made it impossible for my mother to return.''

''So why punish Dante? How is any of this his fault?''

''He knows about me. He knows I exist.''

''No—''

''Yes. We met, Zoe, years ago as children. We traveled to Buenos Aires, my mother and me. I was seven and she took me to my father's house. We rode a bus for three days to get there from the mountains, and then we had to walk a long way from the bus station to this big house in a barrio I'd never seen before. The houses there were all so big. They looked like palaces with the big windows and wrought-iron fences.''

He drew a breath, studied the paper in his hands before shaking his head. ''The walk from the bus station made me very tired. I remember how hungry I was, how thirsty, but Mama told me not to complain but to be happy because I was going to my papa's house.''

"She rang the doorbell and I'll never forget what it looked like when the front door opened. There were big bunches of balloons everywhere and a mountain of wrapped gifts on the table. I could hear music in the house and children laughing. I'd been tired but I suddenly was excited. I thought Mama had brought me to play.''

Zoe felt a knot form in her belly. She held her breath for what might come next.

"My father came to the door and he was not happy to see Mama or me. He yelled at her and dragged her out the front door. She tried to push me toward him and he hit her. He hit her very hard but she didn't make a sound. I remember holding on to her legs, trying to keep her from falling and I looked up at my father and saw the devil—''

"Why the devil?''

He shrugged. "Only the devil would hurt a woman that way.'' He shook his head, raked his hand through his black hair, his face lined with silent pain. "Before we could go, a little boy in a red party hat ran to the door. He'd come crying to his papa because it was his birthday and he couldn't have a second piece of cake. He already had blue icing smeared on his mouth and yet he wanted more.''

Tension rolled from Lazaro in great dark waves. "I'd been shivering, holding up Mama, and this spoiled boy cries over not getting more cake.'' He swallowed, fought for control. "I'm glad Tino didn't take me. I'm glad I had to make it on my own. I don't take anything for granted. Not even the time I've had with you."

Zoe felt a silent sob form within her and yet she couldn't cry, couldn't speak, couldn't reach out to him. She understood he hurt and she hated what he'd been through, but it wasn't all right for him to hurt others. It wasn't acceptable for him to inflict more pain.

The limousine drew before a tall, stately house with three stories and dozens of elegant paned windows.

"This is it," he said as the driver stepped around.

She slid to the edge of her seat, glanced out the open door to the house with its formal front door and pair of pruned topiaries. "I don't know what to say."

"I guess there's nothing to say." He opened his door, stepped out. "I'll walk you up."

"I don't think that's a good idea."

"I'm not afraid."

But no one answered the door, not even a maid or butler. They waited, too, and tried again every few minutes, but ten minutes passed and no one came.

Zoe's heart lifted. She was glad.

Glad.

She didn't understand this, didn't understand herself, but she knew one thing, and that was that she was thrilled she didn't have to say goodbye…yet.

She turned on the doorstep and faced him. He stood down a step and they were almost eye-to-eye although he still had an inch or two on her. "I guess you're going to have to take me with you," she said.

His eyes met hers. He nearly smiled. "I'm sorry."

"Liar."

His lips twisted. "All right, I'm not sorry. I don't want to say goodbye. I don't know that I'll ever be ready to say goodbye."

Ten minutes after leaving Dante's house, the limousine pulled in front of a tall, very modern hotel. The blue-gray granite gleamed in the sun. The chauffeur opened the back door. Sunlight streamed into the car.

"We're here," Lazaro said, scooping up the newspaper and stepping from the black car. Outside he turned and extended a hand to Zoe. "My meeting is in a half hour. I have just enough time to get you settled."

The hotel was the latest in ultra-sophisticated, ultra-expensive accommodations. Lazaro didn't just have a luxurious room reserved, but the entire top floor of the hotel, a huge, private, four-room suite.

He must visit often, too, Zoe surmised as everyone in the hotel from the doorman to the concierge greeted Lazaro by name, and with obvious respect.

They were whisked to their suite, the rooms decorated in combinations of blues, reds, and dashes of black. It was a bold scheme, very strong, much like Lazaro himself.

It wasn't until the bell captain carried Zoe's suitcase into the master bedroom and Lazaro opened the closet revealing a row of suits and shirts that Zoe realized this was his own suite. *He lived here.*

"You live in a hotel," she said, as the door closed behind the bell captain.

Lazaro shrugged. "I own the hotel. Why not?"

"You own a hotel?"

"Plus three others in Argentina, one in Uruguay, two in Chile, and the new one under construction in Brazil."

She sat down on the edge of the bed, touched the quilted spread, feeling increasingly disoriented. "You don't own these with Dante, do you?"

"No. They're part of my corporation."

"Dante doesn't know you have your own company."

Lazaro smiled but the smile didn't reach his eyes. "He does now."

She felt strangely ambivalent again. It was always like this on her emotions, a constant tug-of-war, her loyalties always pulled. "I would have thought most of your wealth was tied up in Galván Enterprises."

"The opposite is true. I have very little invested in the Galván corporation—" He was interrupted by the distinct ring of a phone. He took the call, finished it moments later after having only uttered a half dozen words. "I have to go, but I'll be back before dinner, in three, maybe four hours."

"Don't worry about me. I'll be fine here. You have a TV, and I have my book. Time will pass quickly."

"I can make arrangements for one of the women from my travel desk to take you out shopping and sight-seeing—"

"Please don't. I'd prefer to stay here, really. I'm not that social. At home I'm alone most of the time."

"All right, if it's what you want." He kissed her, lightly on the lips, but from the warmth in his eyes she knew his feelings were much more intense. "I'll see you in a couple hours."

Lazaro leaned forward in his chair and hung up the phone in his downtown office. A two-and-a-half-hour conference call, a new personal record, he thought, rubbing his jaw and staring blindly at the notepad where he'd scribbled numbers, phrases, names as he, the American investors, and the board members of Galván Wireless hashed out the crucial points in wireless telecom acquisition.

Dante hadn't participated in the call. Dante wasn't taking Lazaro's calls. Dante wasn't going to accept the takeover attempt sitting down.

He was fighting back. He was fighting to save what was left of his corporation.

Lazaro had to admire him for that.

Lazaro lifted the notepad he'd been writing on and stared at the scrawl on the page. Among the numbers, phrases and terms, he saw the name Zoe.

Zoe Collingsworth.

She hadn't been part of the plan. Lazaro hadn't even known she existed when he decided he'd carve up Galván Enterprises, rendering the mammoth corporation helpless, useless, and prove to Dante that he, a nothing and a nobody from a poor part of town, could rise up and challenge one of Argentina's most wealthy and powerful families.

That Lazaro, without financial means, without private elementary schools, without an old family network, could become someone just as smart, just as successful, just as influential as Dante.

That he could match wits with Dante, and win.

Win.

Tomorrow, or the next day, or the one after that, he'd win. He'd own Galváns's assets. He'd control Galván Wireless. He'd dismantle Galván Enterprises. And then what?

Lazaro dragged his finger across Zoe's name, across the black ink on the white, lined paper. Zoe.

He wanted to see her. He wanted to be with her. It was that simple.

Business over, mission accomplished, all he wanted was Zoe.

He took her to dinner that night to a glamorous city supper club. She let him order for her and his menu choices delighted her. He also ordered an exquisite champagne that tickled her nose and filled her with warmth.

She felt Lazaro's gaze. He'd been more silent than usual tonight. "Are you all right?" she asked.

"Yes."

"You're not saying much."

"Words won't help us, though, will they?"

The backs of her eyes burned. The waiter cleared their dessert plates and she struggled to give the waiter a thank-you and a smile.

Lazaro was right, of course. Thank goodness he had a way of bringing her back down to earth. Wouldn't do to let her imagination carry her away. There wasn't going to be a happy ending for them.

"I should call Dante's house. I'd meant to," she said, reaching for the champagne glass and then pushing it away again. Earlier she'd loved the way the cool champagne fizzed its way down, warming her stomach and sending flickers of fire through her veins, but now she couldn't handle the bubbles, the lightness, the sweetness. She couldn't handle anything beautiful at all.

"We can call now," he said.

She pressed her nails to her palms, fighting tears. "Is that what you want to do?"

"It's the right thing."

She felt pulled between her past and her present. She could hardly hold the tears back and they burned her eyes, burned her nose and throat. "You've never done the right thing. Why start now?"

He flinched, a muscle pulling in his jaw. "I'm trying to protect you, Zoe."

The flickering candle accented the hard, lean planes of his face. She reached across the table and touched his mouth, his chin. She loved the feel of him. He was big, hard, strong. Yet he was also dangerous. He still posed a threat to Daisy and she didn't know how to reconcile herself to that. "You're not protecting me if you hurt people I love."

"Zoe—"

She sat back. "Why can't you stop this takeover? Nothing's official. No deal is signed."

"But it is official. The news went public yesterday, it was all over the papers. Dante has been informed. It's happening, Zoe, whether you like it or not."

Her stomach cramped. She felt a rise of nausea. As angry as she was with Dante, she couldn't bear to think of how he must be feeling now. "If your mother were alive—"

"But she's not. And that's the whole point. I won't let her be forgotten, either."

Zoe blinked, reached for her champagne, needing it now. "Isn't there another way to remember her? Can't you do something that would honor her—"

"I am!"

She tipped the glass against her mouth, drank the dry French wine with the wealth of bubbles. *What a mess,* she thought. *This whole thing...*

He reached out, touched her arm, slid his hand around her fingers. "Before me, no one in my mother's family finished high school, much less graduated from college. I not only attended college, I earned a master's degree in the States, from Stanford University, on the West Coast."

"You've achieved so much. Why can't that be enough?"

His hand slipped away from hers. "Maybe my success came too easy."

"Building the business couldn't have been easy."

He shrugged. "It didn't seem hard."

"You must have worked endlessly."

"I made some sacrifices."

He'd made more than some, he'd made many, she thought, understanding that he couldn't admit all that he'd given up in his quest for success. He was thirty-seven and he'd never married, never had children, never settled down. He'd lived alone and fought his way to the top by the skin of his teeth.

Looking at his grim expression now, she knew it must have been a long, lonely battle.

Her heart twisted yet again. She couldn't reject him and yet she couldn't accept him. There was no peace on this one, no peace at all. "Do you like Buenos Aires?" she asked softly.

"I live here."

"But it's not home?"

He looked as though he were about to answer and then he clamped his jaw, swallowed roughly, his cheekbones growing more pronounced. "No."

"Where do you call home?"

His fingers traced the edge his coffee cup, his eyes narrowed in concentration. "I don't."

"I'm sorry."

He lifted his head, his silver gaze meeting hers. "Don't pity me. I don't want it. Not from you."

The horrible sadness was back, sadness for him, sadness for both of them. "I don't pity you. I can't pity you." *I love you.*

"I wish life was different, *corazón.* I wish I was different, then maybe things could have been different for me and you."

She felt as though the air was slowly being

squeezed from her. "I hate talking, I hate all these words."

"Then let's stop talking. Let's dance."

"Tango?" she protested, glancing toward the dance floor.

"I'll teach you."

He led her through the dark, crowded supper club toward the softly lit dance floor. Zoe moved blindly, aware of nothing but the warmth of his hand and the hard strength of his fingers wrapped around hers. She felt possession in his touch, felt something so real and so alive it made her want to weep.

Life with Lazaro would be big, real, consuming. Life with Lazaro would be unlike anything she'd ever lived before.

She wanted to tell him she loved him. She wanted to lose herself in him for just tonight, but looking up into his face, seeing the shadows in his silver gaze, the words died within her.

Words wouldn't help. There was nothing either of them could say.

On the dance floor he half spun her out and then spun her back into his arms, bringing her close to his chest, his hand firm in the dip of her spine.

It felt like he'd lit a fire beneath her skin. Every place he touched, burned. Every nerve ending pulsed. She felt him step between her legs as he turned her, creating an even closer intimacy.

She clung to him as he spun them across the polished wood floor, footsteps fast and intricate in time to the sultry music, yet the guitar played her heart, and the melancholy sound of the accordion was matched by the cry of the violins.

The music captured her emotions perfectly. Love and longing. Hope and fear. Happiness and despair. In his arms, she felt everything.

He kissed the side of her neck, the same spot he'd touched over a week ago when she'd first arrived. "I shall never forget you, *corazón*. I shall never not love you, my heart."

"Ssssh, don't say anything," she whispered, her breath catching, her voice husky. "I can't bear to think. I just want to feel you, be with you."

His fingers played her spine even as the guitarist played the strings on his instrument. "Then tonight I shall try to pretend, too. I shall try to live as though I'm the right man for you."

And he was the right man, she thought, closing her eyes and resting her cheek on his chest, right now no one had ever been more right. No one had ever made her feel more beautiful, more desirable.

She allowed him to move her, lead her, and felt the delicious connection between them grow. She wanted him. He wanted her. The desire grew, becoming larger, fiercer, taking shape as hunger. "Let's go back to the hotel," she whispered, touching her mouth to his cheek. "Let's go to your room."

"And do what?" he answered, drawing her even closer to him so that she felt the ridge of his chest and the hardness of his hips. He wanted her.

Heat shimmered within her. *"Everything."*

In the sweet darkness of their hotel room they made

love fiercely, as though the intensity of their desire for each other would consume them if they didn't love deeply, passionately.

Swept away by the pleasure of being in Lazaro's arms, Zoe didn't hear the phone ring. It wasn't until Lazaro lifted his head and gazed toward the phone that she heard the ring. Then, and only then, was she drawn back to reality. She hadn't been in reality, she'd been on the moon in the most beautiful dance with him.

"It's three-thirty in the morning," Lazaro said, voice raspy with passion. "Who would be calling now?"

Zoe felt a chill. Good phone calls never came in the middle of the night. "I think you better answer."

He slid out from beneath her warm damp body to take the call. He didn't stay on the phone long. He spoke quickly, tersely, and then hung up.

Snapping the cell phone shut, he moved to the bedside table and turned on the lamp. "You better get dressed. Daisy's in labor."

CHAPTER EIGHT

THE hospital was only fifteen blocks away, but reaching the hospital was the easy part. Getting information was next to impossible. With Dante in the delivery room with Daisy, the nurse at the information desk wouldn't, or couldn't, tell them anything.

Zoe paced the blue and cream maternity waiting room chewing her thumbnail, trying not to think the worst but failing miserably. Dread and fear wrestled within her and she felt a gnawing sense of guilt. She felt responsible for this.

If Daisy lost the baby…

"Don't think that way." Lazaro's voice reached her, interrupted her silent stream of worry.

Seething, she stopped pacing and faced him. "How do you know what I'm thinking?"

"It's all over your face. But you didn't do this, you didn't create this—"

"What was I doing? What was I thinking? I should have been with her. I should have been there for her." Turning away, she retreated to the window.

"How could I do this?" But she wasn't speaking to him as much as herself. How could she have let this happen? Daisy had practically raised her. Daisy was always there for her. She should have put her sister first. "I screwed up."

''You didn't screw up. We didn't do anything wrong. We were together, that's it.''

''I'm sorry, I can't ignore this, or deny my part. I know what I did. I know what I didn't do. I can't pretend I'm innocent. I should have been with her. Period.''

In the clear light of morning, in the cool sterile hospital, she saw him, and her, and it made her stomach turn inside out.

What was she thinking? Why hadn't she been thinking?

She gazed out the window into the courtyard below. The sun was just rising, casting fingers of rose and gold across the stone pavers and the delicate statue of a mother and child. But instead of the coral roses blooming in the courtyard, she saw the fat cabbage rose wallpaper in her dining room at home, remembered the framed photos lining the stairs, the pictures of young Daisy and a mother she'd never known.

Daisy's and Zoe's mother had died in childbirth.

Zoe's voice shook. ''If she loses this baby I'll never forgive myself.''

''You aren't responsible for her—''

''Get out!'' She spun around, pointed at the elevator. ''You don't belong here—''

''She's right, you don't belong here.'' It was Dante, standing at the double doors leading to the delivery room. ''Leave now.''

Zoe rushed toward him. ''How's Daisy? And the baby? Tell me she didn't lose the baby.''

But Dante didn't answer, his attention focused on

Lazaro, his jaw granite-hard. He drew a short, sharp breath. "I trusted you," he gritted, ice in his voice, rage glittering in his eyes. "I trusted you, embraced you, made you part of the family."

Lazaro barked a laugh. "I was never part of the family."

"I tried—"

"You never treated me as a brother," Lazaro interrupted harshly, upper lip curling. "I was an employee, a hired hand, nothing more than that."

Dante wheeled back a step. "Is that what you wanted? You wanted to be my *brother?*"

"I *am* your brother."

It was Dante's turn to laugh, coldly, unkindly, his voice ringing too loud in the sterile waiting room. "Maybe in blood, but not in spirit."

Zoe couldn't bear this. "Dante, please."

But he ignored her. He marched on Lazaro, his fury tangible. "If you wanted to be family, come to me as family, open your arms in love, and yes, I'll accept you. But you took a knife and you plunged it in my back. What kind of homecoming do you expect?"

Long-buried pain shadowed Lazaro's eyes. His expression turned bleak. "You had a lifetime to welcome me and you never did."

"I don't know what you're talking about."

"You do."

Dante shook his head impatiently, unwilling to listen to this. "What kind of stories have you told yourself? What kind of lies did your mother make up?"

"Bastard!" Lazaro swore, lunging at Dante.

Zoe threw herself between them. "No! Lazaro, no, don't do this!"

But Dante reached around Zoe, his temper raging, too. "No, *you're* the bastard."

Lazaro ducked, pulled Zoe out from between them, pushing her behind him. "You want to fight? Come on—"

"Lazaro, Dante, no!" Zoe saw Lazaro's tight fists, knew his strength. Dante was nearly as big but she had no doubt that Lazaro was the better street fighter.

They weren't listening to her, too embroiled in their own bitter feud. "I was there," Lazaro continued. "I was at your house, I know the life you lived and you can't pretend you didn't know I existed."

"I had a suspicion, yet I never knew it was you."

"Why didn't you look for me? Why didn't you try?"

"I had my own life, and my own problems—"

"That's right, the poor aristocratic Galváns—"

"Stop it!" Zoe screamed, clapping her hands over her ears, hearing more than she'd ever wanted to hear. This was awful, this was impossible. "What about Daisy? We're here for Daisy. How can you do this now?"

Lazaro wheeled away first, ashen, sickened. He wiped his mouth off, drew a ragged breath. "I can't believe I wanted to be part of your family. What was I thinking?"

"Indeed," Dante answered hoarsely, color darkening his hard cheekbones. He stared Lazaro down, disgust written in his eyes and press of his lips.

"You'll never be part of us, and you're not welcome near us."

"Good, because I don't want you. I don't want any of you."

Zoe felt cold, all the way to her bones. *"Lazaro."*

But Dante's rage grew. "You know, Herrera, you're the worst kind of blood. You're the kind that festers and poisons and kills. Daisy nearly died last night and I'll never forget the hell you've put us through."

Zoe's legs buckled. "Stop—"

Lazaro reached for her but she pulled away, too horrified, and trembling.

Her rejection shook him and he stared at her for a long, tense moment. Shadows gathered in his eyes, shadows of confusion and pain. But this time she couldn't reach out to him. She'd had enough. She had to finally take sides.

"You better go, Lazaro." Zoe's voice broke. "Now."

His silver gaze narrowed. "So this is how it is."

She couldn't bear this. She knew he was suffering but he'd chosen his weapons and his weapons hurt. "Yes."

He swallowed hard, a muscle pulling at his jaw. "Fine. I'll go."

"Do," Dante answered fiercely. "Go quickly, before I call the police."

Lazaro disappeared into the elevator, and even as the doors shut, other doors opened and a nurse appeared wearing hospital scrubs. Zoe heard a baby wail, the newborn's cry high and thin, piercing in its intensity.

The nurse gestured toward Dante. "*Por favor.* Your wife wants you."

The nurse led them to a private recovery room. The light was dimmed and the room, although spacious, felt stark. Daisy was awake though, and she lifted her head when Zoe entered the room.

"Zo…" she croaked, smiling weakly. She lifted a hand, fingers bending, entreating Zoe closer.

Daisy had purple shadows beneath her eyes and her pale face looked drawn. Carefully Zoe sat down on the edge of the bed, noting the tubes taped to Daisy's hand and the tubes to her arm. "Are you okay?" Zoe asked.

"I'm fine." Daisy glanced toward Dante who stood just off the foot of her bed and mustered another small, weak smile. "Just a little tired, that's all." She reached out to touch Zoe's hand. "How was the flight? When did you get in?"

So Daisy didn't know Zoe had been with Lazaro. Daisy didn't know about the arrangements Dante had made. Daisy knew nothing about Lazaro. What a web of lies…

Zoe swallowed the lump in her throat, still in turmoil over what she'd witnessed in the waiting room. "Not too long ago," she fibbed, hating the position she'd been put in.

"And Dad?"

"Dad's fine. But more importantly, how are you? And what about the baby?"

The door to Daisy's room opened and a nurse

wheeled in a small glass isolete. "Your son," the nurse said, pushing the isolete with the tiny infant toward Daisy's bed.

"A boy?" Zoe choked, turning around to gaze with wonder at the baby. A miniature mask was delicately taped to his face but he looked beautiful. Small but beautiful.

"Oxygen," Daisy explained, fingers outstretched as if she could touch the baby through the glass. "His lungs are still underdeveloped but the doctors don't think there should be any serious problems later. The pediatrician calls him a little miracle."

"Your baby," Zoe repeated softly. "You have a baby. Daddy will be so happy."

Daisy tried to smile but she couldn't quite do it. "Daddy will finally have his boy."

Outside, in the hospital parking lot, Lazaro sat behind the wheel of his Mercedes sedan. The engine was on, the car in drive, but he couldn't accelerate, couldn't move at all.

It was all out in the open now. No more hidden agendas. No more secrets. No more games.

It was what he'd always wanted it to be, brother against brother until the better brother won.

Lazaro knew the moment he moved publicly against Dante that the relationship would end, but he hadn't expected to feel loss.

He did feel loss. Tremendous loss. And shame.

It crossed his mind as he sat with the car idling and the morning sun glazing the hood of his car, that maybe, just maybe, he'd made a terrible mistake.

*   *   *

Daisy needed rest and Zoe joined Dante in the hospital cafeteria for coffee. They both ordered a breakfast roll and Zoe took a couple bites of hers but Dante didn't touch his.

Dante pushed aside his small plate. "I'm sorry, Zoe. I'm sorry for everything."

"Tell me you didn't ask Lazaro—"

"I did. I was wrong."

"Damn straight you were." She swallowed hard, utterly bewildered by all that had happened in the past week and a half. "How could you?"

"Daisy," he answered simply. "I was worried about her."

"You were worried that *I'd* hurt Daisy?"

He shifted, shoulders shrugging. "The engagement to Carter."

"There was no engagement. Just because he asked me didn't mean I said yes."

"He was spending a lot of time at the farmhouse."

"He was kind to Dad."

"Zoe, he's a crook. Lazaro—" Dante broke off, ground his teeth together, struggling to contain his temper. "He wouldn't agree to help me until after he looked into Carter's record." Some of his tension eased. "Carter has quite a record, Zoe. I don't think you're safe there, at the house, with Carter around."

"I'll keep that in mind." She stared at him hard. "But don't try to make decisions for me, and don't think you know what's best for me. I love Daisy, and I love you, but I'm not a kid anymore—"

"You're only twenty-two."

"Twenty-three," she corrected.

"When?"

"Three months ago." Zoe sighed, shook her head, her long fair hair held back with a simple hair band. "I understand how you wanted to protect Daisy, I feel the same way, too, so I won't tell Daisy what you did, but you have to respect my decisions from here on out."

"Agreed."

She looked at him for a long moment, gathering her courage, trying to find the right words without being unnecessarily hurtful. "What's happening with your…business?"

"My business," he repeated softly, mockingly, before lifting his cup and taking a swallow. "What do you think?"

He didn't say more. He didn't have to.

Zoe practically lived at the hospital over the next couple of days. She sat with Daisy as much as possible, even when Daisy did nothing but sleep. Yet her heart wasn't easy. She thought of Lazaro frequently, but just thinking of him made her feel like a traitor.

As she and Dante switched places at the hospital two days later, Zoe asked Dante for news regarding the takeover. "I'm still fighting," he said, lips twisting into a cynical smile.

"Daisy never talks about it. She does know, doesn't she?"

"She knows, but I think she's in denial. She considered Lazaro a friend. I don't think she understands how he could do this to me."

"I'm sorry. I wish I could have stopped him—"

"How?"

If he'd loved her, he wouldn't have done it.

If he loved her.

She blinked, eyes scratchy. Dante noticed her watering eyes. "You should go back to the house, get some rest. You look tired."

"No more tired than you," she answered. But she did take the waiting limousine back to the house, and she did try to nap. Unfortunately, sleep didn't come. Her brain continued to race and her thoughts haunted her.

She couldn't stop thinking about Lazaro. Couldn't stop missing him, either.

Zoe changed into white jeans, a comfortable knit top and laced up her white sneakers for a walk. She enjoyed being outside and liked walking in Dante's elegant neighborhood.

Reaching the corner, she crossed the street and entered a small public garden. Suddenly she was surrounded, or it felt as though she was surrounded, as a reporter thrust a microphone in her face and another man turned a camera and light on.

The man with the microphone rattled off questions in brisk, flawless English. "Can you confirm your relationship with Lazaro Herrera, Miss Collingsworth? And does your family know, or is it a clandestine affair?"

Zoe froze. She lifted a hand to shield her eyes from the bright camera light. "I don't know what you're talking about."

"The pictures ran in this morning's paper. Pictures of you dancing the tango."

She struggled to follow. The reporter's English was impeccable. It was her brain that wouldn't function. Dancing the tango? Why, the only time she'd danced the tango was that night with Lazaro at the supper club, and that was nearly a week ago. "I'm sorry, there must be a mix-up. The pictures must be of someone else."

"You're Zoe Collingsworth, Count Dante Galván's sister-in-law?"

Zoe opened her mouth, closed her mouth, panic setting in. Daisy couldn't find out about this. Daisy couldn't handle this. Daisy didn't need this on top of everything else.

"It's true that you and Lazaro Herrera are involved?" the reporter persisted.

"No, it's not true."

"And the pictures in the paper?"

She had to get out of here. Had to find Dante. "I can't answer that. If you'll excuse me."

She ran home, blindly, breathlessly. Dante was already there. He had a newspaper with him, one of the English versions printed for the ex-patriots living in Buenos Aires. She held her hand out for the paper and he gave it to her without a word.

On the front page was a large color photo of Lazaro and Zoe dancing. Zoe stared at the photo. A lump filled her throat. "This is bad," she whispered.

"Yes."

"How do we keep this from Daisy?"

"She's already seen it. She gave the paper to me."

Zoe paced the hospital corridor that afternoon in despair. Daisy hadn't been unkind to her, nor had she said a single harsh word, but Daisy was shattered, not just by the very public photograph, but by late-breaking news that Galván Enterprises was close to destruction.

The stock had plummeted since word broke about the hostile takeover. Investors were desperately trying to get rid of their shares and Dante, having trusted Lazaro to manage the corporation's holdings, realized now, too late, that Lazaro had deliberately weakened the company just for this.

There was no way the corporation could gracefully recover, no way Dante could wield any effective power.

Zoe's sense of guilt grew. She should have stopped Lazaro. She could have stopped him if she'd only tried harder. But it wasn't too late to do something now.

Shaking, she stood in the hospital corridor and dialed Lazaro's cellular number. She expected to get his voice mail but he answered. "Lazaro, it's Zoe. I have to see you."

He picked her up from the hospital in his large silver-tone Mercedes sedan. Inside the car she stared at him. His face looked fierce, hard. New lines were etched next to his eyes and mouth, accenting the hump in the bridge of his nose.

Pain washed through her in waves. She still felt so many intense and conflicting emotions. "I want to hate you," she said. "I want to hate you for what you've done."

He just stared out the windshield, his expression

shuttered. "Let's go for a drive," he said at last. "Let's get some privacy so we can talk."

He pulled away from the hospital and they wove through city streets until he reached a quieter residential neighborhood.

She watched him as he drove, wondering why she felt so exquisitely alive, so exquisitely sensitive when together with him. She shouldn't feel this way. Shouldn't care.

He pulled over in front of a park, killed the engine. But he didn't speak.

Zoe wanted him to say something. She wanted him to defend himself or apologize or somehow make it better, but he didn't.

Her heart twisted with fresh hurt. "You told me you'd try to protect Daisy, you told me you'd protect me."

"I wanted to protect you—"

"Then why didn't you do it? You promised me you would. I want you to keep the promise you made me. Find a way to fix this."

"I can't undo what's been started—"

"But you can find an end to it. I know you can, Lazaro." She loved him. Still. But she couldn't bear to love a man like him, couldn't bear to be in love with someone who would injure and wound. "They can't lose everything. You must do something. I know you can. I know you. If anyone can fix this, you can."

He sighed, frowned. His dark eyebrows pulled together. "There is a way—"

"Fine. Do it."

"You'd be part of it."

"Anything, as long as you make this nightmare go away."

There was no gentle way to break the news, Zoe realized later as Daisy let out a howl of rage.

"Marry Lazaro Herrera?" Daisy's voice rose, and she staggered up from the chair in her hospital room. "Absolutely not. You can *not* marry him, Zoe. I forbid it."

Zoe knew this would be difficult and tried to stay calm now. "You can't forbid it, Daisy. This is my choice, my life."

Daisy's long silver-blond hair danced as she shook her head. "Don't do it, Zo, don't even think about it."

"It'll save Dante's company."

"Dante would rather go broke."

Zoe didn't believe it, not for a minute. Maybe right now, in the heat of battle, Dante imagined he'd prefer to starve than concede victory to Lazaro, but later, after things calmed down, Dante would realize there were too many people dependent on him to let his pride get in the way. This wasn't just about taking care of Daisy and the new baby, he had his three sisters to think of, as well as an extravagant step-mother in need of frequent cash infusions.

"You don't want Dante to lose everything," Zoe answered softly. She clasped her hands together, trying to hide the fact that she was trembling. Confronting Daisy was the hardest thing she knew how to do. It was impossible standing up to her. Daisy had always been Zoe's heroine.

"Dante won't lose everything. He's fighting the takeover—"

"Making the Galván stock prices fall faster." She got to her feet, approached Daisy with outstretched hands. "I understand the stock has already lost two-thirds of its value. If Dante continues to fight the takeover he'll lose it all."

"He's smarter than that."

"It's not an issue of intelligence, Daisy, it's timing. Lazaro hit Dante when Dante was weak—"

"So how can you even consider marrying him? Lazaro Herrera is evil. Malicious. Manipulative—" Daisy's voice fell away as she drew a strangled breath. "My God, he's destroying us for what? *His father's sins?* Why make Dante suffer for something that isn't his fault? What did Dante ever do to Lazaro but support him…empower him? How could Lazaro betray Dante like this?"

Zoe's stomach hurt. She felt sick all the way through her. "I don't know."

"You can't marry him."

"We've already set the date."

"No!"

Zoe winced at the pain and outrage in her sister's voice. They'd had fights before, disagreements before, but never anything like this. "Daisy, give him a chance to make things right."

"Give him a chance? A chance to do what? Destroy the rest of us?" Daisy's expression turned stricken. "I hate him. I hate what he's doing to Dante. I hate what he's doing to us and I'll never feel differently. Never!"

"We will fix this—"

"You can't fix this one, Zo. And you can't marry him. If you do, you'll have cut yourself off from us."

"Daisy," Zoe pleaded, "please don't say that."

"You marry him, and you're not part of this family."

Tears filled Zoe's eyes and she clasped her hands together to hide the trembling. "Not even if I can help save Dante's company?"

"No! No, no, no." Daisy pounded her fist on the door. "If you marry, you marry for love, and you marry for happiness, but you *don't* marry for money!"

"Maybe I do love him."

"You can't mean it."

"We've already applied for the license and gotten the blood test. The ceremony is Saturday."

Daisy's chin lifted, her blue eyes glacier-cold. "Then this is goodbye."

Desperation swept through Zoe. She'd never felt panic like this. It was as if a frigid wind had blown in and it chilled Zoe's blood. "Tell me you're joking."

"I'm serious. You marry Lazaro Herrera and we're finished." Daisy sounded hard, impossibly harsh, but then her lips quivered as she fought for control. "Don't do it, Zoe, please, Zoe, don't do it. For my sake, if nothing else."

Zoe's heart ached. It felt as though it would burst any minute. "I love you, Daisy."

Daisy ground her teeth together, even as tears welled in her eyes. "Listen to me, Zoe. You marry him, and we're finished. Do you understand?"

CHAPTER NINE

LAZARO looked gorgeous in his tuxedo. With his black hair and hard, chiseled features he looked like pictures of Hollywood leading men. As he stood at the end of the cathedral, just below the altar, Zoe thought of the rugged film star on the red carpet, smiling for the cameras.

He was smiling for the cameras now.

It was their wedding and he was playing it the way they'd agreed. They'd scripted the wedding, scripted their reunion, scripted the merger between Galván Wireless and Argentine Wireless, a merger which still left Lazaro in charge but had stopped the Galván stock from plummeting and protected Dante's personal fortune.

Lazaro had been amused by her insistence on making it a real wedding. She'd told him she was only getting married once, so it might as well be authentic.

Now she knew why he'd laughed at her. Standing in the Buenos Aires cathedral, wearing a twenty-thousand-dollar designer gown, while four hundred guests waited for her to walk down the aisle was not exactly a personal, authentic ceremony.

There was nothing remotely personal, or authentic about this ceremony. Daisy hadn't come. Dante had been coerced into standing with Lazaro at the front of the church, something which made Zoe cry privately with shame.

This wasn't her idea of a white wedding, even though her hand-beaded gown was white, and lavish white lilies and orchids cascaded from the ends of each dark wood pew.

Zoe began to tremble in her new white satin heels. She clutched her bouquet tighter, pressed her elbows to her waist. She could feel the clear sequins and pearls stitched to the fitted white gown, feel the weight of the long silk train and the stiff veil anchored to her jeweled tiara.

She was dressed like a princess but felt like a fraud. This wasn't how it was supposed to go, this wasn't how her wedding was ever going to be. She'd meant it when she and Daisy promised years ago to only marry for love. She'd meant to keep the vow.

Zoe felt a bubble of hysteria rise and it was all she could do to hold it in. She couldn't run away, even if she wanted to. She couldn't disappear...where would she go?

As if sensing her panic, Lazaro turned, and looked down the long carpeted aisle to where she stood at the back of the cathedral. Late afternoon light flooded the massive stained-glass windows, turning the church interior into a living Chagall. The enormous vases of lilies scented the church with an almost overpowering perfume.

His gaze found hers and held. From twenty feet away she felt his confidence and his intensity. He'd never struck her as arrogant, she realized, just determined. He didn't strike her as arrogant now, just more determined.

He was the kind of man who'd move mountains if necessary.

He'd moved those mountains, too.

As his gaze continued to hold hers, she felt a ripple of sensation in her middle followed by a burst of heat. He was the most physical man she'd ever known and she responded to him helplessly, instinctively. Even now she reacted to him as if he were the only man alive. The only man left on earth.

Blinking, she held back gritty tears, forced herself to concentrate on the tall taper candles on the altar and the huge organ pipes on the wall. She'd never seen a church so big before, had never even entered a cathedral before. What was she doing, getting married here? Who did she think she was, marrying like this?

The bouquet in her hands was heavy, the opulent sweetness of the lilies making her head start to ache. She didn't think she could stand here another minute but suddenly the organ swelled, filling the cathedral with rippling sound. The sound was too big, too strong.

Her cue.

It was her turn to move, to walk down the aisle and join Lazaro at the front of the cathedral.

Zoe didn't know how she reached the altar. Her legs were shaking like mad, her pulse racing too fast.

The priest was talking, speaking first in Spanish and then in English, and yet it might as well have been Greek. She understood almost nothing. Time seemed to pass in slow motion.

Lazaro was staring down at her, his expression hard, almost mocking. She wanted to run from the hardness in him, wanted to escape.

''Zoe Elizabeth Collingsworth, do you take this man to be your lawfully wedded husband,'' the priest's voice pierced her panic, forcing her attention back to the ceremony. ''For better or worse, richer or poorer, in sickness and in health...''

Zoe didn't hear the rest, her eyes riveted on Lazaro's face.

He was so angry with her.

He didn't have a right to be angry. He'd started this.

So why was she marrying him?

To save Galván Enterprises. It was the only way to ease the backlash against Dante and his family. The only way to forge a relationship between Dante and Lazaro.

Unity. Family. Commitment.

Zoe pressed down through her white satin heels, locked her knees for courage.

This wasn't a hostile takeover, but a family merger. It wasn't a collapse of Galván Enterprises but a new union of two brothers' fortunes.

''Till death do you part,'' the priest intoned.

She caught the flicker of Lazaro's eye, caught the tightening of his jaw.

She swallowed. ''I do.''

And Lazaro smiled without a hint of warmth.

*   *   *

Ceremony over, they rode in the back of the stretch limousine, heading from the city cathedral to the exclusive country club on the outskirts of Buenos Aires.

"Are you happy?" Lazaro drawled, sitting opposite her.

She didn't even try to smile. She couldn't.

"It's what you wanted," he continued, filling the silence. There was an edge to his voice, anger in his voice. "The wedding was your idea. You insisted on it."

She couldn't look at him. "You were going to ruin their lives."

"It was just money."

"Don't say that," Zoe whispered in the dark, her voice choked. Her chest felt tight, the air strangled in her throat. "You know Dante's whole family depends on him. His sisters, his stepmother, Daisy and now the baby."

"We all make choices."

"Yes, and you chose to wound." Head aching, she closed her eyes, tipped her head against the window's glass, longing to disappear. How was she possibly going to make it through the reception?

Lazaro's voice cut through her thoughts. "You chose to play the sacrificial lamb, Zoe. You came to me."

No, he felt absolutely no remorse.

She opened her eyes, looked at him, watched as the shadows flickered across his face, highlighting the high, carved cheekbones, the long broken nose, the full sensual mouth. His features were so hard, so distinct, they were beautiful.

She was reminded of that first night, in the helicopter, when he'd stolen her from the airport and whisked her to his home on the pampas. Her heart tightened, chest tender. Even at his worst, she was still drawn to him. "I wasn't going to watch Dante and Daisy's world crash down on them."

"But this isn't just about them," he said flatly. "This is as much for you. You didn't want to lose me. You couldn't let go."

Her head snapped up, her lips parted in denial but she couldn't find her voice. He was right, of course. She couldn't hide anything from him, not even her feelings.

Especially her feelings.

"Am I supposed to feel sorry for you?" she choked, nails pressed to the crusted silk skirt. Their limousine was creeping through the city traffic and nearly at a standstill.

"*¡Por Dios!* Sorry for me? *No.* I have what I wanted. Everything I've ever wanted."

She flinched inwardly, his words striking her as though they were sharp stones. Turning away, she looked out the tinted window, her gaze scanning the crowded sidewalks. "And what is it you wanted?"

"You."

She shook her head in denial. "You don't want me."

"Don't want you? Zoe, I love you. I've loved you since the first night I met you. I knew then you'd change everything, and you have."

"Words," she whispered. "They're just words."

Outside the car she spotted an elderly man clinging

to a newspaper kiosk, his handsome but weathered face lined with pain.

She drew a small, shallow breath, feeling her emotions dance dangerously on edge. "Why would you love me, Lazaro? What do you love about me?"

He leaned forward, caught her by the upper arms and lifted her off her seat onto his. Her silk skirts swished and whispered as she slid onto the leather next to him and he lifted her face to his, his fingers spanning her cheek and jaw.

"Why would I love you?" he repeated huskily, thumb stroking the curve of her cheekbone, his narrowed gaze studying her closely. "Just look at you."

Her heart ached. "If this is about beauty—"

"Not just beauty, although you're beautiful, but all of you. Your kindness, your sweetness, your spirit, your strength. You are what I'm not. I'm drawn to you, like a moth to a lamp, or darkness to light."

"Don't say it like that."

"But it's true. What am I but shadows and secrets? What do I want but revenge?" He covered her mouth with his, parting her lips with the pressure from his, and drank in air from her lungs.

Zoe felt him draw her breath into his mouth and her head grew light. She placed her hands against his chest to steady herself, and was vividly reminded of his strength. His chest was all warm, hard, taut muscle beneath his white shirt and she flashed back to two weeks ago when they were at the hotel, making love. She flashed to the feel of being in his arms, naked against his flesh.

She loved him, and yet he scared her. She'd never

felt so confused in all her life. Tears seeped beneath her closed eyelids and trickled out.

Lazaro lifted his head, caught a tear with a tip of his finger. "You're crying."

"I don't understand you."

"You don't need to understand me."

Her chest squeezed tight and her throat ached with tears. "How can you say that? I'm going to live with you. I've married you."

"But you're not going to change me. You can't hope to change me. I am what I am, and this, Zoe, is me."

She couldn't answer and she felt his sudden impatience. He lifted her from her knees and returned her to her seat. "Don't cry," he said, "it's your wedding day."

His cool voice and his mocking words made her feel horrifyingly alone. What in God's name had she done?

Averting her head she again spotted the elderly man in the blue blazer. He'd made his way from the newspaper kiosk to the street corner, where he now clung to the streetlight.

The man staggered a step, swayed on his feet, and staggered another. His progress was painfully slow and he'd pause frequently to draw a deep breath and run a trembling hand through his thick white hair.

Zoe felt sick watching him. He reminded her of her own father, reminded her that life was short and time fleeting.

She wanted to help the man outside but didn't know what to do, didn't know how to help.

Suddenly Lazaro opened his door and climbed out. Black tuxedo jacket flapping, he approached the elderly man, and placed a hand on the man's shoulder.

Lazaro's forehead furrowed as he spoke, and Zoe watched, her heart beating hard, and doubly fast. She hadn't realized that Lazaro had seen the man, she hadn't realized that Lazaro would notice someone else's pain.

Her heart turned over yet again.

Lazaro lifted a hand, signaled to a taxi. Placing a hand under the other man's elbow, Lazaro walked the gentleman to the waiting taxi and assisted him in. Lazaro drew bills from his wallet, handed the money to the elderly man and the taxi pulled away.

Lazaro returned to the limousine and the limousine moved forward.

Lazaro didn't look at her and Zoe didn't know what to say. *If he wants to talk, he'll talk,* she told herself, hoping he'd talk, hoping he'd explain.

The limousine made a right at the corner, zigzagged through more traffic before merging onto the expressway. But Lazaro didn't explain.

Dante arrived at the reception late, appearing nearly two hours after the dinner had started. He didn't make any excuses as he took a seat at Zoe and Lazaro's table.

Lazaro said nothing to Dante, but she cast her brother-in-law a worried glance. "Is everything all right?"

Dante lifted the glass of wine sitting untouched until now at his place. "Why shouldn't it be?"

"Well, Daisy—"

"She's not happy."

Zoe chewed on the inside of her lip. "But the baby, he's fine?"

"He's good."

Zoe forced a smile. "Good."

The orchestra had begun to play and photographers approached the table and snapped photos of Dante, Lazaro and Zoe together. Their smiles were tight and uncomfortable, but all were careful to maintain the facade of togetherness for the cameras and guests.

Photographs over with, Zoe danced the first dance with Lazaro but neither spoke. Lazaro was more distant than ever and Zoe was afraid if she tried to talk that she'd end up in tears, and tonight she couldn't, wouldn't, cry. Not for anything.

Dante asked Zoe to join him for the second dance. With the media clustered on the edge of the dance floor, he partnered her in a slow waltz, the elegant Strauss waltz a sharp contrast to Dante's barely concealed hostility.

"Things will get better," she said quietly, "I promise."

Dante's jaw jutted. "Don't make promises you can't keep."

"I do intend to keep them, especially this one. I'll find a way to make it up to you."

"You can't. This is between Lazaro and me. It's always been between him and me."

She heard her name called, turned, and blinked as a flashbulb exploded. "Quite a crowd," she murmured, finding it hard to concentrate on the one-two-three box steps she'd learned back in junior high school when Daisy had insisted Zoe take ballroom lessons as part of her etiquette training. It was a six-week charm school course on Saturdays, and Daisy had driven Zoe to the lessons herself, wanting Zoe to know the things she didn't know, already wanting Zoe to have experiences Daisy wouldn't have.

"Lazaro would put on a show."

"He's happy, and I really do believe he loves me—"

"He can't love you because he doesn't know how to love anyone."

"I don't agree."

Dante's expression turned grim. "I'm not going to let you do this. I won't let you throw your life away. You're going to leave with me. We'll go now—"

"You must be joking!"

"Not at all. We'll walk out together. No one will stop us, not with reporters and photographers here. My car is out front waiting. Don't worry about your things, we'll get you whatever you need tomorrow."

"I can't, Dante, I can't do that to him."

"Why not? He'd do it to you if the price was right."

She saw his lips twist in a hard, cynical smile and suddenly saw Lazaro in him, saw the resemblance between them. It wasn't the eyes, but the mouth. They had the same curve of lip, and the same wide, sensual mouth. Even the way they smiled was the same. Which was probably why no one had noticed the resemblance before. Dante smiled frequently. Lazaro rarely did.

Yet Lazaro was beautiful when he smiled. He was like another man altogether. A man with hopes. A man with dreams.

As they danced, they passed a cluster of photographers. More camera flashes popped, bright blue-white blinding bits of light.

As she blinked, he drew her to the edge of the dance floor. "We're going to walk now," he said flatly. "Once we break through the crowd, just keep going. My driver is in front, waiting. He knows we're coming. Daisy knows we're coming—"

"No." She couldn't do this. Couldn't walk and leave Lazaro here, alone, not tonight, not at their reception.

"Zoe, if you don't leave now you might not get the chance again."

"I know." But she saw from Dante's puzzled expression that he didn't understand.

She couldn't explain it, couldn't justify it, couldn't find any rational explanation, but she loved Lazaro. When she looked at Lazaro she saw someone Dante didn't see. She saw Lazaro the great, Lazaro the tender. She saw a man who needed love and she loved him.

It was that simple. "I'm not walking out on him," she said, eyes burning as she doggedly lifted her chin. She untangled her hand from the crook of his arm. "This is my life. This is my future. I want to be with Lazaro."

The music ended and the orchestra had yet to start a new piece. Dante and Zoe stood at the edge of the dance floor.

''He'll destroy you, Zoe.''

Her chest felt tender and she blinked. ''I don't be-lieve it. He's not like that—''

''That's what I thought, too, until he proved me wrong. I thought I knew him. I thought I knew what kind of man he was. But he isn't like you or me. He isn't like anyone you've ever met. He'll hurt you badly—''

''Bad-mouthing me on my wedding day, brother?'' Lazaro mocked, appearing beside them. He looked relaxed, his expression deceptively friendly, yet Zoe felt his tension and saw the cynicism in his brittle silver gaze.

Dante didn't even flinch. He turned to Zoe, took her hands in his. ''Come with me. I'll get you home, I'll put you on a plane back to Kentucky.''

Zoe's chest felt far too tender and bruised. ''Good-bye, Dante. Thank you for coming tonight.''

Dante's amber gaze turned frosty. ''I'm not leaving without you.''

Her smile hurt. Her heart hurt. This was worse than painful, this was hell. She loved Dante and Daisy but she couldn't live for them, or through them. ''But I'm not going with you,'' she answered as gently as pos-sible. ''I'm not leaving Lazaro. Please, don't do this here, now, not on my wedding day.''

''Zoe—''

''No, Dante. Don't make it worse than it has to be.''

Dante looked exhausted, and spent. ''You'll call, if you change your mind.''

''Yes, but I won't change my mind.''

Dante shrugged. He'd done what he could. "You know where to find me, Zoe, should you need me."

She didn't see Dante leave, didn't see him cross the ballroom or walk out the white-paneled doors, her vision blinded by scalding tears.

Neither she nor Lazaro spoke. The musicians had started up again and the dance floor was filling fast. A peal of laughter sounded from the far side of the room and Zoe glanced that direction, from where the laughter had come.

"You could have left," Lazaro said roughly. "You could have walked just now."

She turned slowly to face him, and met his gaze. "I know."

His expression shifted, suspicion giving way to bewilderment. "Why didn't you?"

"I made you a promise. One's word must mean something. You taught me that."

"He's right, you know. I can't keep you here, I can't make you do this."

"No one is making me do anything."

He lifted a black eyebrow. He didn't understand. She wasn't sure she did, either.

"What am I supposed to think?" he asked, his voice deep, husky with emotion he couldn't express.

He hated this, she realized, he hated not understanding, not knowing, not being able to predict. Far better that she reject him outright than give him hope…

Suddenly she didn't want to argue anymore, didn't want to waste time on bad feelings, or family feuds. This was her wedding. This was her night.

A waiter carrying a tray of champagne flutes passed close by. Zoe lifted two flutes from the oval silver tray and handed one to Lazaro and kept the other glass.

As she handed the flute to Lazaro, her fingers brushed his and she felt a ripple of warmth, expectation, as well as pleasure.

She suddenly felt older. Stronger. More sure of herself. She wanted to be here. She wanted to be with him. ''To us,'' she said quietly, lifting her goblet.

He didn't answer immediately. He gazed down at her, the same puzzled expression that had shadowed his eyes earlier back. ''You could have had a great life.''

She stared into his silver-gray eyes. ''I'm going to have a great life.''

''Zoe—''

''You're not the only one that feels deeply. I feel things deeply, too. I feel things deeply for you.''

His face could have been an iron mask. There wasn't a twitch of muscle anywhere, not a change of expression. ''You're too beautiful. I don't deserve you.''

''We all deserve to be loved,'' she answered gently. ''Even you. Especially you.''

Lazaro pushed the stiff white veil from her bare shoulder, his fingertips sliding over her collarbone and her smooth satiny skin. His eyes darkened, the silver-gray turning to smoke. ''You give me hope, Zoe. You make me believe.''

Her head tipped back, her throat revealed, the candles and dim light from the chandelier dazzling her eyes. "You should believe. You must believe in us. I do."

He was beautiful, she thought, and his face with its hard lines and sensual lips made her crave to touch him, to be part of him. Her stomach clenched, belly tightening with need. She wanted to feel him again, to be part of him again, to have him make her his.

His hands on her breasts. His mouth on her lips. His body taking complete possession of hers.

"Then to us," he murmured, drawing her closer to him, nearly crushing the full, beaded skirt. "I will drink to us."

She brought the goblet to her mouth, tasted the crisp barely sweet champagne, the color pale gold, elegant, the stuff weddings were made of.

But she didn't need the champagne fizz to add to the bubbles inside of her. Something else was happening here, something new and strong.

She stood on tiptoe and pressed close to him. Her lips briefly touched his. "I love you, *corazón*."

There was pain in his eyes. "Don't—"

"It's true. I do love you. You're part of my heart now."

He drew her completely against him, held her close, so close she could feel the steady drum of his heart and the heat of his body. "I don't know what to say. I can't find the right words."

Tears smarted her eyes and her throat burned. Zoe felt warmth rise up in her like a hot-air balloon, filling her chest with tenderness, protectiveness. "Then let's not talk. Just dance with me. And if you forget how, I'll show you."

CHAPTER TEN

THE reception was still in full swing when she and Lazaro made their escape. They were driven from the country club back to Lazaro's hotel.

The curtains were open in the living room and they had a magnificent view of the city, lights sparkling under a bright full moon.

Lazaro slid off his tuxedo jacket and dropped it on the back of the white couch. Zoe watched as he unfastened the top buttons on his dress shirt, leaving the collar open and his tanned throat exposed. He rolled up the sleeves of his shirt without either of them saying a word.

Her stomach felt like a bundle of nerves and she pressed her hands to the sides of her skirt. She felt shy all of a sudden, and inexperienced. They were married now. Married.

"Turn around," he said, moving toward her.

She did as he told her, drawing a swift breath as his hands settled on her shoulders. He slid his hands beneath the stiff veil, lifted the starched fabric and kissed her neck.

Just that one touch of his mouth to her neck sent rivulets of feeling through every limb.

He kissed her again and then slowly began plucking the pins from the tiara. "Your head must ache. This crown weighs a couple pounds."

"It is a little heavy," she admitted, thinking that it didn't take much for him to waken her senses. She responded so instinctively to him, so attune to his touch, his heat and energy that just being near him made her want so much more.

Carefully he lifted the tiara and veil from the top of her head, before sending it onto the couch along with his tuxedo jacket.

His hands moved to the tiny hooks on the back of her gown. "I want you, *corazón*. I want you, all of you."

He kissed her nape and she dipped her head, her loose hair brushing her cheek. She loved the way he touched her, loved the way he made her feel. When he kissed her like this, and held her tenderly, it felt like it was just the two of them alone, the two of them alone against the world.

Slowly he began to undo the dozens of tiny hooks hidden in the seam of the gown. As he unfastened each hook he kissed her back, kissing each vertebra all the way down until he reached the top of her bustier, and then he touched his tongue to the skin exposed above the delicate satin and silk lingerie.

The feel of his tongue on her bare skin made her shiver. She nearly cried.

"You're so sensitive," he said, sliding his hands down her sides, from her ribs to her small waist, fingers spanning the narrow width.

"Tonight, especially," she agreed, eyes closing as he continued his quest, slipping her wedding gown over her slim hips, down her silk-covered thighs until the expensive jewel-crusted gown lay in a decadent puddle at her feet.

With the gown discarded he slid his hands back up her legs, working from the instep to the ankle, along the inside of her knee.

Zoe sucked in air as his mouth replaced his hands on her thighs, his breath warm against her heated skin, his tongue playing across the fine white silk stocking encasing her thigh.

"I want to kiss you," he said, stroking the inside of her thigh.

She needed kissing, she thought, feeling rather frantic. Her mouth definitely needed attention. "Yes."

And then his mouth touched her at the apex of her thighs, his lips caressing her through silk panty. Her legs trembled, and she grabbed his shoulders.

His breath teased and tickled through the silk, and the sensation of his mouth against her made her half crazy with need. It was amazing to feel so much at one time, from the snug pressure of her boned corset to the tug of her garter strap to the heat of his mouth and hands.

She dug her hands into his hair and savored the feel of his thick, crisp hair, the feel of his mouth against her most tender part of her body. "Lazaro," she choked, voice husky and full of longing.

"What's wrong?"

"I want...I want..." Passion colored her voice. She didn't even sound like herself. "More."

"Like this?" he asked, caressing the back of her thighs, the curve of her bottom.

Exactly like that.

She could hardly breathe, hardly think, mindlessly aware of the heat of his hands against her sensitive skin and the intimacy of his mouth to her sex. It was, this was, the sweetest of pleasures.

He made everything feel good. He made everything right. He could do anything to her, she thought, dizzy with need, and she'd enjoy it. All she wanted was to belong to him, to be made part of him.

Heat burned through her, staining her cheeks. ''Let me touch you,'' she begged.

''No, this is my turn to love you.''

She couldn't say another word, or think another coherent thought. He was kissing her through her silk panties again, blowing air against her skin and then tracing the shape of her with his tongue. His breath made her shiver. The tip of his tongue nearly made her scream. She arched helplessly as one of his hands slipped beneath the elastic on the panty leg, pushing aside the tiny scrap of silk to kiss her again.

Zoe dug her hands into his hair, needing him, needing to touch him, needing to hold him as close as possible. They'd made love before but never this, nothing had ever been like this. She couldn't imagine anything ever being more intimate. If she wasn't his before, she was now.

Her body began to tense, the coiling of desire building into growing waves of pleasure. Yet as much as she enjoyed his mouth on her, as much as she liked the feel of his warm mouth on her warm wet body, she wanted to be face-to-face, chest-to-chest.

''I need you in me,'' she whispered, gently breaking free. ''Make love to me, Lazaro, make love to me now. Please.''

Lazaro didn't need more encouragement. He'd wanted her all night, had hungered for her for weeks. He'd felt empty without her in his arms, in his bed. But it wasn't sex he wanted as much as love.

Her love.

He needed her love more than he needed air.

Swinging her into his arms, he carried her into the bedroom and together they undressed him before he pushed her back onto the bed, against the mountain of snowy-white pillows. Her hair gleamed in the dark, the lightest shade of gold, and he knelt over her, seeing yet again the beautiful perfection of her face, the straight nose, the wide thickly lashed eyes, the mouth.

The mouth.

He covered her mouth with his own, touched his tongue to hers, and drank her in.

''I love you,'' he whispered in Spanish. ''I will love you forever and ever.''

When they finally made love he buried himself deeply in her, filling her, settling into her as though he'd come home for the first time in his life.

He'd never felt so much joy, or peace, and his eyes burned. He was unable to fathom the depth of his emotion. He felt like a man given a second chance, a new life.

He could do anything.

He could be anything.

He could even make her happy.

Lazaro moved in her, deeply, slowly, prolonging the contact, heightening the intensity, allowing the pleasure and sensation to build. He was with her. He was in her. He was giving all of himself to her. They'd never be as close as they were now.

"Lazaro," she whispered, touching his face, bringing him even closer.

"Yes, *corazón?*"

"I love you."

"I know. And I'll never take you, or your love, for granted. I swear."

Later, after they were warm and relaxed, Zoe turned to him, gazed at him in the dark, trying to see his face, wanting to see his eyes. "The man we saw today, downtown…"

"Yes?"

"You put him in the cab."

Lazaro shifted slightly, his arm moving to circle her waist. "He was in pain."

Zoe felt a rush of fierce emotion and suddenly knew she'd done something right by loving him.

They'd come from different places, faced different obstacles, and yet they needed each other. Were meant for each other.

Leaning over, she kissed his mouth, his beard grazing her chin. She cupped his cheek, loving the feel of him. Loved his strength and hard edges. "Thank you for helping him." Her voice came out husky, roughened by emotion, exhaustion and passion.

She could feel his jaw tighten against her palm, his cheekbone growing prominent. "Don't thank me. It was the least I could do."

"I kept thinking it could have been my father."

His jaw tightened yet again. "I'm sure he was someone's father, just as he was someone's son."

Later, after she'd fallen asleep in his arms, Lazaro lay awake for a long time, well over an hour, weighing the past, considering the future.

He'd heard the longing in Zoe's voice when she mentioned her father. She missed him.

For her, the ties to her family were very tight, very binding. He wasn't comfortable with ties like that, had never been connected the way she was connected, yet he was beginning to understand that he and Zoe were different, had different needs.

Had he done the right thing, marrying her? Had he hurt her more than he'd helped?

He didn't know, didn't want to know, in case his motives hadn't been pure.

They spent the first week of their honeymoon doing little besides savoring each other's company. There were dinners out, visits to nightclubs and theater, shopping trips that lasted all day and resulted in bags and boxes of the newest designer fashions.

Lazaro had the means to dress Zoe and he loved to watch her model evening gowns and stylish pantsuits, casual daywear and skimpy swimsuits.

As she slowly twirled in front of the boutique's full-length mirror, Lazaro applauded. He loved her in silver and gold, loved her in white, loved her naked and eager beneath him.

Zoe caught his eye and her cheeks bloomed pink. Shyly she wagged a finger at him. "I know what you're thinking."

"I can't help wanting you. I won't ever stop wanting you."

She placed her hands on her hips, an unconsciously provocative pose in the snug silver-sequin gown. "Are you sure this isn't just about sex?"

His gaze swept her flushed face, taking in her full soft mouth, the bright laughing eyes. He'd never lived until he met her, never felt like a man at all. "If it is, then why does my heart hurt?"

Her smile faded. "It shouldn't hurt your heart to love me."

"It's only because I'm so happy. I'm not used to this kind of happiness."

"Lazaro…"

"I'd lay down my life for you, you know that, Zoe. I'd give up everything for you. You're the best thing I've ever known, the best part of me."

Her eyes filled with tears and she crossed the floor to kneel next to him. Her heart ached with an emotion she couldn't articulate, and barely understood. "I'm not the best part, *we're* the best part," she whispered urgently, hands against his thighs, her heart thumping too hard, as if she'd been running too fast. "It's not you or me, it's us. Us together. Us making a life together."

He reached toward her, stroked her hair, let a long loose blond tendril slip through his fingers. "I think it's too good to be true—"

"No."

"I think sometimes it's wrong to have so much happiness, especially as it has come at the expense of others."

He was talking about Dante, talking about her family and she drew a painful breath. ''It will all work out, Lazaro, I am sure of it.''

''You must miss Daisy.''

Her heart squeezed tight. She did miss Daisy, and she missed Dante and the baby, too. She had a nephew she'd never been allowed to touch or hold and she wanted to sit with him in her arms and stare into his little face and learn all about this new person.

But that wasn't going to happen, not now, not the way things were. ''We'll get this resolved one day,'' she repeated firmly, voice thickening. She didn't want to think about what she'd given up; she had to believe that they'd get through this, find a way to mend the fences. ''Things always work out in the end.''

He smiled but the smile didn't touch his eyes. The expression in his eyes was sad, troubled. ''Sweet Zoe,'' he said, kissing her forehead. ''So innocent.''

They returned to the hotel and although Lazaro had made dinner reservations at one of Buenos Aires's most exclusive clubs, Zoe begged to stay in and just lounge at home. ''We could rent a movie, or watch TV,'' she said, ''and room service could send up hamburgers and ice cream.''

''What about your new dress? I thought you'd want to show it off.''

The silver-sequin gown was breathtaking but Zoe didn't want to show off. She just wanted to be alone with Lazaro, wanted to sit close and simply be held. ''I'd rather just sit on the bed with you.''

They ordered hamburgers and French fries and rented a movie from the hotel cable system. Halfway through the movie, the phone rang. Lazaro glanced at his watch and, muttering something under his breath about the late hour, answered the phone.

He spoke rapidly in Spanish and hung up less than a minute later. "Good thing we stayed in," he said, reaching for his cast-off shirt and pair of trousers. "Dante and Daisy are here, waiting to see us downstairs. They're on their way up now."

Zoe grabbed her jeans from the side of the bed and the fun pink and orange tie-dyed shirt Lazaro had bought her a few days ago. She had just enough time to run a brush through her hair before the doorbell sounded.

Emerging from the bathroom, she looked at Lazaro. His gaze met hers and he must have seen her fear. "It's okay," he said quietly. "We're together, remember?"

Dante and Daisy had come without the baby. Daisy wore a leather coat and Zoe offered to take it but Daisy declined. "I'm fine," Daisy said flatly. "Besides, we're not staying that long."

Zoe felt a pang.

"Dad's missing," Daisy said without preamble, no emotion in her voice. She kept her cool blue gaze fixed on a point just beyond Zoe's shoulder. "I thought you should know."

Zoe turned to ice. She balled her hands with difficulty. "How long has he been gone?"

"Nearly twenty-four hours. He disappeared from the nursing home."

"Why didn't you call me sooner?"

Daisy's head jerked and her hard gaze met her sister's. "I didn't think you cared anymore."

Zoe felt the words sink in and they sliced through her, as though Daisy had cut her with a knife. Zoe's lips parted and yet she couldn't breathe, couldn't speak, the pain too deep. "Of course I care! I love Dad. I love *you*."

Daisy gritted her teeth, her jaw jutting whitely. "Dante's flying out tonight to join the search. He already has Clemente working with the police."

"I'd like to go, too," Lazaro said. He turned toward Zoe. "We both want to go."

Zoe nodded. "Just give us a minute to grab a few things and then we can leave together."

They flew out that evening, less than two hours later, but the drama was over by the time their plane landed in Lexington.

Clemente had found Bill Collingsworth. It seemed that Zoe's father, after leaving the nursing home, walked the twelve miles back to the family farm in his robe and pajamas.

Zoe, hearing the news not long after landing at the Lexington airport, burst into tears. She'd been sick with worry, fearing the worst. "Dad just wants to be at home," she said, wiping away the tears and trying to get some control back. "I don't blame him, either."

"I can't imagine it's an easy adjustment," Lazaro said, taking her hand.

She swallowed hard, around the lump blocking her throat. "He's spent his whole life on the farm. He's used to having plenty of space, lots of fresh air. Of course he'd go home. That's where he belongs.''

As the limousine sailed past the familiar bluegrass meadows and pastures, Zoe felt a bittersweet ache. She loved Kentucky but this wasn't home anymore. Not for her father, and not for her.

On the flight she'd overheard Dante and Lazaro discussing the farm. Lazaro knew Dante was heavily invested in the farm and she sensed it was only a matter of time before Collingsworth Farms was sold.

As the limousine turned down the private road leading to the farm, the white fences and distant farm buildings emerged through the early morning mist. She'd never loved horses the way Daisy loved horses, but Zoe did love the land and old Victorian farmhouse. She loved the history that rooted her here.

The limousine rounded a bend and the old two-story Victorian farmhouse came into view. Zoe leaned on the door to get a better look. She'd been gone a month but it felt like years.

Her gaze swept the house and garden, inspecting everything, wanting to see what had changed and what remained the same. The front steps had been painted. The railing fixed. The climbing rose's tender new canes were tied to the trellis at the side of the house. Clemente had done a good job with upkeep. Thank goodness they'd had his help.

The car parked and Zoe dashed out of the back and up the front stairs before Lazaro or Dante could climb out.

Her father was in his room, sitting in the overstuffed chair that had once been her mom's favorite chair. He looked so small, so lost.

"Dad."

He turned, saw her in the door. His forehead creased. "Is that my baby?"

"Yes, Daddy. It's Zoe."

"Oh, Zoe, where have you been?"

She hugged him until her arms ached, hugged him until the horrible coldness in her middle went away. "I love you," she said, kissing his cheek, and drawing a footstool close to sit next to him. "I missed you."

"Don't leave me anymore."

Her eyes burned and yet she forced a smile. "Let's not worry about anything right now, okay? I'm home, and I'm here and I want to know what you want for dinner."

"Pot roast."

She blinked back the scalding tears, telling herself she couldn't think about tomorrow, couldn't think about anything but today. "Okay. Pot roast it is."

The next few days passed quickly for Zoe. It was wonderful being home. It felt wonderful being back in the old farmhouse. She'd only been gone four weeks but it had felt like forever.

While Lazaro and Dante spent time with Clemente on the farm, going over the farm books and discussing the new stallion barn, Zoe sat with her father and read to him and tried to keep him busy.

Afternoon sunshine poured through the double-hung windows, catching the crystals of the chandelier and throwing tiny rainbows of color on the smooth painted walls. She loved the house, loved the high ceilings, the thick crown moldings and painted casing. She loved the view of the pasture from the front veranda and the twenty-year-old pink climbing rose that would soon begin to bud.

This was home. It'd always be home. Even if she couldn't live here anymore.

They'd been at the house for nearly a week and Zoe knew Dante and Lazaro were both anxious to return to Argentina. Neither had said anything to her but she couldn't help feel their growing restlessness. Soon they'd want to go home, and she'd return with them.

But her father…what about him?

During dinner that evening she knew Lazaro watched her, and knew that he, too, was considering the future.

His corporation and career were in Buenos Aires. She couldn't ask him, or expect him to move to Kentucky, and yet her father's entire life had been lived here, on this land, in this house. Collingsworth Farms was a four-generation horse farm. It'd been started by her father's great-grandfather in the early part of the twentieth century. How to let it all go? How to walk away from a history of love?

Dinner over, she steered her father upstairs to get him ready for bed. Twenty minutes later, as she padded barefoot down the stairs, she heard Dante and Lazaro's voices coming from the kitchen.

"It doesn't make business sense to keep the place, the farm barely breaks even." Dante was speaking, and Zoe hesitated in the hall. "But I'm not in a hurry to sell, either. This is still Daisy and Zoe's home."

"And Bill's," Lazaro added. "He obviously wants to be here. I think he should be allowed to remain here."

"I do, too."

Lazaro attempted a laugh. "Then we agree on something."

There was a moment's silence and then Dante coughed, cleared his throat. "We might agree on Collingsworth Farms, but that's about it. I can't continue with this, Lazaro. I can't maintain this—"

"Continue with what?"

"This. Us. You and me working together. It's a charade and it doesn't sit right with me." Dante sounded tired, his words flat, weary. "It's not the way it was…before."

Zoe pressed her hands to her stomach, knots filling her middle, tension spreading through every limb. She hated this. Hated the sides, the conflict, the discord.

"No, it's not," Lazaro tersely agreed.

"I want out."

"But it's your company."

"*Was*. It's yours now."

She closed her eyes, and leaned against the door frame, assailed by guilt all over again. She'd married Lazaro, loved Lazaro, but it hadn't changed anything. The marriage might have saved Dante's wealth, but it hadn't saved his pride. It hadn't fixed the hurt, or healed any of the deep wounds.

She felt the weight of the problems, felt worn out

by the problems. Her father. The farm. The rift between families.

She'd spoken to Daisy only once in the past five weeks, and it'd been the night she and Dante came to the hotel with news that their father was missing. What had happened to her family? What had happened to all of them?

Lazaro abruptly appeared, turning the kitchen corner, a platter in his hands, a dish towel across his shoulder. He nearly tripped over her in the dark. "Zoe!"

She blushed, realizing he knew she'd been standing there, eavesdropping. "Dad's in bed," she said in a breathless rush. "Hopefully he'll have a quiet night."

She felt Lazaro's gaze search her face, felt the strained silence between them.

But he didn't speak. His mood changed, shifting into something quiet, and distant.

"Let me take that," she said, reaching for the platter. "I know where it goes."

"So do I."

She took the platter anyway, needing the task to give her something to do. Anything would be better than standing there, feeling helpless, feeling hopeless.

She and Lazaro didn't need words. They could read each other's thoughts, read each other's emotions without saying a word. And right now they both knew they hadn't escaped the past, or the pain. Instead of starting a new life together, they realized at that very moment that they'd only succeeded in dragging heartbreak into the future with them.

Later that night, after they'd gone to bed, Zoe

reached for her husband in the dark. Wordlessly they made love, slowly, passionately, straining against each other for greater intimacy. The intensity of Zoe's orgasm shattered her and she clung to Lazaro afterward, her body quivering, her heart tender, tears in her eyes.

She loved Lazaro desperately but felt a dark cloud moving over them. Something was going to happen, something was going to change but she didn't know what, and she didn't know when.

She tried to hide the tears from Lazaro but she couldn't. He rolled her onto her back, and lifted her hair from her damp face. "You feel it, too," he said softly.

She shook her head. "No."

"You do. We both do. I think we both know this is impossible."

She wasn't sure what he meant, but she heard the sorrow in his voice. She pressed her mouth to his bare shoulder, fear growing, rising, threatening to consume them. "Nothing's impossible," she answered fiercely. "Nothing is ever impossible if we believe."

CHAPTER ELEVEN

NOTHING is ever impossible if we believe.

Zoe's words rang in his head and Lazaro wanted to believe her. He wanted to cling to her optimism, find some peace in the future but he didn't have that kind of faith. Especially not in himself.

He held her closely, drew the blanket over them as if the blanket could protect her. Deep down he knew better. The person she needed protection from was himself. "I will never make you happy."

"You already have."

Lightly he stroked her satin shoulder, the smooth expanse of back. He wanted to remember this, wanted to remember the softness of her skin, the sweetness of her nature. He'd never loved anyone this way before and knew he'd never love anyone so intensely again. "But I've driven a wedge between you and your family. You and Daisy were once so close, now you can hardly be in the same room together."

She didn't immediately answer, kissing his chest and pressing her cheek to the curve of muscle above his heart. "One can't have everything in life."

He swallowed hard. The weary wisdom in her voice hurt him. She was only twenty-three. She shouldn't have to feel this way now. Shouldn't have to know so much at such a young age. "You deserve better, *corazón*." He cupped the back of her head, the long silky hair cool and slippery beneath his fingers.

He'd never loved anyone so much.

He'd never needed anyone so much.

She shouldn't have had to choose between her family and him. He'd forced her to choose, too. He'd wanted to isolate her from those that knew her, from those who loved her. He wanted her to be like him.

Alone.

Lazaro swallowed again. Felt the huge lump return, blocking his throat.

He'd ruin her life, had already come frighteningly close to ruining the lives of those she loved.

"Lazaro." Zoe shifted in his arms, lifting her head to look at him.

He felt her concern. It felt gentle, soft, a velvet throw and for a man who'd never felt plush-velvet fabric until nineteen, velvet was a dream.

Her palm touched his cheek, moved tenderly across his face to brush his mouth. "What's wrong? Tell me."

Air squeezed into his lungs. His chest ached. He'd never not love her. Never not want her. He kissed her fingertips. "Tonight I couldn't stop looking at you. You're the most beautiful woman I've ever known—"

"I was wearing jeans and a purple T-shirt!"

"Yes, and you had your hair pinned up on top of your head and you were humming while you mashed potatoes. I loved it. I loved watching you. I've never seen you laugh so much before. You don't need jewelry and designer gowns. You just need your family around you.''

She shifted and slid across him, covering him, her long hair spilling like a silver-gold curtain around them. ''I need you,'' she answered, dipping her head, touching her mouth to his. ''I love you.''

His heart twisted. ''And I love you, my Zoe.'' But this time love might not be enough.

It was time to return to Buenos Aires and despite Zoe's efforts, and Dante's pleading, Bill Collingsworth refused to even consider leaving the house again. He wouldn't discuss returning to the nursing home and outright rejected the suggestion of moving to Argentina.

''I live here,'' he said flatly, ''I'm staying here. In my house.''

Zoe knew he couldn't care for himself but Lazaro suggested having Clemente move into the house until they could find a suitable live-in nurse. It wasn't a perfect solution but it was better than forcing Bill into returning to the convalescent home.

It was the last morning of their visit to the farm and Zoe had finally finished packing. The suitcases were loaded into the limousine's trunk and all that remained were the goodbyes.

But Zoe didn't know how she was supposed to say goodbye to her father this time. She didn't even know when she'd return next. Lazaro said she could visit as often as she liked, but things could happen, things did happen and she worried about the changes that would take place between visits.

Her father met her at the front door, dressed in a chambray work shirt and khakis. With his shoulders thrown back, and his silver-streaked hair combed, he looked amazingly like his former self, as though the Alzheimer's hadn't eaten away his memory and cognitive powers.

His piercing blue eyes focused on her small travel bag she clutched in one hand. "Where are you going, Daisy?"

"I'm Zoe, Daddy."

"That's right. Zoe, my baby. Where are you going?"

She couldn't do this. She couldn't leave him now. He might not even remember her when she came back. "On a trip," she answered brokenly.

"Will you be gone long?"

"Not too long, I hope." Her voice cracked again, and she dug deep for strength. She couldn't fall apart now, it would only worry him, make him uneasy.

She pressed down into the heel of her boots, locked her knees, squared her shoulders. She had to go, her future was with Lazaro, but it nearly killed her to walk away from her past. "Clemente has the phone number where I'm staying. If you need anything..."

"I won't need anything."

"But if you do—" and she couldn't continue, couldn't get around the lump filling her throat. "Call me, Dad, please?"

"All right, baby."

She was in his arms, holding him tight. He patted her back, slowly, firmly, as though she were a child again. This is how it'd always been with them. Before his illness. Before the problems. Her heart ached, wanting the impossible, wanting things simple again.

But they'd never be simple again. She'd grown up.

As he released her she stepped back, and she smiled through her tears. "You raised me right, Dad. You did a good job. I hope you know that."

He smiled back. "That's good. That's my girl. I'll see you tonight at dinner."

But there was no seeing him tonight at dinner and she knew it.

Back in Buenos Aires, Zoe and Lazaro tried to settle into a routine but Lazaro wasn't easy, and couldn't seem to relax.

At first Zoe thought it was the time change and jet lag when Lazaro left their bed in the middle of the night to go work in the sitting room, but as one week turned to two, she worried about the new distance between them.

They made love less, far less, and when Lazaro did reach for her she felt his tension, felt an anger and despair he refused to acknowledge, much less discuss.

Three weeks after their return Lazaro stopped coming to bed with her altogether. He slept in the small guest bedroom that adjoined the suite and didn't explain his decision, or defend it. He just moved away from her.

Zoe couldn't pretend that the distance between them was a figment of her imagination anymore. There was a problem. A big problem and she didn't know how to solve it.

Zoe desperately wanted to talk to Lazaro about

what was happening between them but each of her attempts to talk was rebuffed. He still took her out to dinner every evening, he still wanted her to dress up and play the glamorous bride, but he didn't want her. He didn't reach for her. Didn't express tenderness anymore.

Zoe didn't know what to do, didn't know where to turn. Three weeks turned to a month and she felt painfully alone, worse than alone. Felt alienated. This was his country, his world, and she didn't belong.

She climbed from bed and slid her arms into her light cotton robe. It was close to three in the morning and she hadn't been able to sleep, worry and fear going 'round and 'round in her mind.

Lazaro sat at the desk in the living room. He was working on his laptop computer, typing away and looked up when she entered the room. ''What's wrong?''

She stared at him, numb, tired, too tired to play this game. ''What do you think's wrong? You don't come to bed with me anymore. You don't touch me anymore. You tell me. What's wrong, Lazaro? What's happened?''

''It's work, that's all. I'm just under the gun.''

''It's more than that,'' she answered quietly. ''Your feelings have changed.''

''They haven't changed.''

''Then why have you pulled away? Why are you so distant?''

''It's nothing personal—''

''Not personal? Lazaro, I'm your wife!''

''And wasn't that a mistake.''

Tears filled her eyes and Zoe's lips parted in silent protest but in the end she couldn't speak. She shook her head, tears clinging to her lashes and returned to the bedroom.

Lazaro stared at the bedroom door which she'd gently closed behind her and knew he should get up, go to her, try to comfort her, but maybe this was better, he told himself flatly, maybe this was the best way.

It would never work long term. He felt too guilty, felt too destructive, and he hated dragging Zoe into his world of anger and revenge and pain. From the beginning he'd wanted to protect her and yet all he'd done was hurt her.

Over and over again.

Lazaro sat for long tense minutes fighting himself, fighting his desire to go to her, fighting his need to hold her and love her. It was a terrible battle, a battle that made his heart burn, but he kept himself there, motionless in the chair, until the fire began to burn out and the desperate craving subsided.

He didn't deserve her love. How could he? He was nothing if not pathetic and low.

Zoe dressed slowly in the morning, her fingers trembling as she buttoned the lime-green silk blouse, and tucked the blouse into the waistband of her cream, linen trousers.

Morning sunshine poured through the bedroom blinds, burning her eyes. She'd cried herself to sleep last night and had cried nonstop since stepping from her morning shower.

How could Lazaro stop caring for her? How could

his feelings change so quickly? He'd managed to shut himself down completely. It was as if he'd forgotten her, pushed her from his heart, and his mind.

She didn't understand. She couldn't understand. She loved him.

Suppressing a cry of anguish, Zoe grabbed her wallet and took the elevator downstairs. Outside the doorman hailed a cab for her and Zoe gave the driver Daisy and Dante's fashionable Recoleta address.

The maid showed Zoe into the formal living room with the high ceilings and beautiful old plaster walls. The fireplace was enormous with the most beautiful pink marble surround.

Daisy entered the living room moments later, wearing faded jeans and a soft buttercup-yellow T-shirt. She was carrying the baby high against her shoulder as though she'd been burping him when informed of Zoe's arrival.

"Am I interrupting?" Zoe asked, rising from the chair she'd taken, self-conscious again.

"He's almost asleep," Daisy answered, standing in the doorway, gently patting the tiny infant's back. She looked thin. She'd already lost all the baby weight and more.

Zoe reached for her wallet. "I can come back—"

"No," Daisy cut her short. "This is fine." But she didn't draw closer and her expression didn't change.

Daisy was so guarded, Zoe thought, feeling an almost unbearable sadness that their relationship had become so strained. That they had come to this.

She and Daisy were strangers.

Just like she and Lazaro were now strangers.

Her stomach in knots, Zoe gripped her wallet tightly. Now that she was here, she didn't know what to say, didn't know how to start talking. Daisy didn't even like Lazaro, why did Zoe think she could possibly come to Daisy with her problems?

Because Daisy had always been there for her before.

Because Daisy was her sister and Zoe loved her with all her heart.

Tears filled her eyes and she realized it was a mistake to come. Zoe rose a second time. "This wasn't a good idea. I should go. I'm sorry I bothered you."

She walked quickly toward the door, passed Daisy and hurried down the black and white marble hall, anxious to reach the front door.

"Do you want to hold him?"

Daisy's question drew Zoe short. She stopped in the hall, facing the door, pressed her wallet to her stomach. *Did she want to hold him?*

Slowly she turned, gazed longingly at the baby. "Yes. Please."

In the living room, Daisy handed Stefan over. The baby had dozed off and his little hands lay folded across each other, as though he were the most angelic child ever born.

Zoe silently marveled that he weighed nothing at all. As she settled him more firmly in her arms, he stretched and sighed, and her heart turned over. "He's beautiful," she whispered, in awe over his miniature perfection. Black hair, nub of a nose, sweet lips.

She couldn't resist kissing his cheek and she breathed in his baby-powder smell.

"You'll be a great mom someday," Daisy said, taking a seat opposite her, her long legs tucked beneath her.

"I hope we have kids."

"Why wouldn't you?"

Zoe couldn't answer. At the moment she didn't see how her marriage would last another month, much less a year. If she didn't reach Lazaro soon, they wouldn't be together long enough to have a baby.

Zoe felt her throat start to thicken. She couldn't tear her gaze from her nephew's face. To sleep so peacefully, to feel so safe...

She glanced up, met Daisy's eyes. "I'm glad you have Stefan. He's so lovely. He's perfect."

Daisy smiled but the smile didn't reach her eyes. "What's wrong, Zo? What's happened?"

Zoe blinked, fought the tears, fought for her control. Tears wouldn't help. Swallowing hard, she found her voice. "It's Lazaro."

Zoe didn't return to the hotel until nearly six, a half hour before Lazaro usually returned from work. But tonight he was already back when she opened the door, sitting on the living room sofa reading the newspaper.

"Hello," she said, closing the door behind her. She felt an odd prickle seeing him home already, seeing him here, waiting for her. It wasn't as if she'd done anything wrong but she felt anxious, strangely defensive. "How long have you been home?"

"An hour or so." He folded the newspaper, set it on the sofa next to him. "I'm sorry about last night."

The sweetest relief surged through her, relief so strong she felt dizzy. "I am, too."

"I want you to be happy, Zoe."

"I am. With you."

He gave his head a slight shake, his jaw tight and she dropped her wallet and keys on the dining room table and moved toward the couch. Leaning over the back of the couch she kissed him. "I'm so glad to see you," she whispered, her heart impossibly tender. "I've felt just terrible."

"I'm sorry." He reached up, cupped her cheek. "Where have you been? I've been phoning the apartment every half hour. I was worried about you."

"Is that why you're home so early?"

"I thought perhaps…" but he didn't finish the thought. He shrugged, shoulders lifting. "At least you're home now."

She took a seat on the couch next to him. "I…I saw Daisy." Zoe tucked a strand of hair behind her ear. "I've just come from her house. I got to hold the baby. He's really beautiful—" she broke off, hearing her babble. At least she felt as though she were babbling. "Do you mind?"

"Mind what? That you saw your sister? *¡Por Dios, Zoe!* I'm glad. I hate what's happened to you two. I hate what I've done—"

She reached over, covered his mouth with her palm. "Let's not talk about it now. Let's just go to dinner, relax, and enjoy each other, okay?"

She was glad she suggested going out. Dinner at Hermes was magical. Lazaro acted like his old self. Charming, warm, attentive. He ordered champagne, toasted her, saying he was the luckiest man alive. She told him about the day she'd spent with Daisy, more about Stefan and how much he'd grown since his birth.

Lazaro listened to everything, half smiling, his silver gaze focused. "It was good to see her, wasn't it?"

She couldn't hide her happiness. "It was wonderful. I've missed her so much." She told him then about the dinner invitation for the next night. "Would you please go with me?"

He looked at her for a long moment, his thick lashes lowering to conceal his expression and then he looked up at her again. "They are not my family, *corazón.*"

"They could be."

Lazaro's expression gentled even more. "I humiliated Dante before all of Argentina. I have nearly bankrupted him. I do not think we will ever be family."

"But we can try. We can start somewhere."

His lips twisted, a small crooked smile, and Zoe saw a weariness in his eyes she'd never seen before. He looked less like Lazaro the warrior and more like Lazaro the defeated. Her heart ached for him, ached for both of them. Her gaze searched his. "Lazaro, we have to start somewhere."

"Maybe."

"Come to dinner with me tomorrow."

He gave his head a rueful shake. "All right, for you, I'll do anything."

After their late dinner they returned to the hotel and made love for the first time in over a week. Lazaro slowly undressed her before loving every inch of her skin, touching, kissing, licking. He made her quiver and melt, prolonging her pleasure to make it more intense. When she finally came, it was with him buried deep inside of her. The orgasm was so powerful she felt as though he'd shattered her and she clung to him during and after, needing his comfort and strength.

"I love you," he whispered, kissing her damp neck, her chin, her still sensitive mouth.

He hadn't said the words in so long that she felt both joy and pain. Zoe nestled closer. "You're sure?"

"Yes. It's the only thing I know for certain anymore."

Lazaro left early for work the next morning. He skipped lunch, not having time between meetings and discussions, and worked straight until four when he poured a glass of mineral water and took a break to stand at the window.

As he stood there, watching the busy street traffic below, he couldn't help marveling at his success. He'd done it. He'd done exactly what he'd intended.

He'd been completely successful, completely ruthless, and he was completely wrong.

Instead of peace he felt only anguish. Instead of pleasure he felt remorse.

He'd done what he'd wanted and it had alienated him from those he wanted—needed—most.

For a brief point in time he almost had the life he wanted. He had Zoe. He had the closest thing to family he'd ever known. For a brief point in time he was in heaven.

He returned to his desk, sat and clicked on his computer. Jaw gritted, he began deleting his personal files from the hard drive, one file after the other.

As he deleted files he swallowed hard against the wretched taste of self-disgust. He'd earned two university degrees, learned complex management theories, built a career, become accomplished in arts and developed an ear for music—for what?

To be alone.

To live alone.

To die alone?

Impossible. Unfathomable. Who the hell was he kidding? This wasn't ever the kind of life he wanted for himself, this wasn't the kind of person he wanted to be. As a kid he worked harder than anyone to succeed, to be accepted, to be liked. As a kid he wanted nothing more than to be...*loved.*

How had hurt and anger twisted him into this? How had loneliness become such a vendetta?

Lazaro paused, pressed two fingers against his brow, the tension in his head nearly unbearable. He wasn't sleeping anymore. Wasn't able to eat. Couldn't rest.

He stared at the last file on his computer, a file marked DG. Dante Galván. Swiftly he deleted this last file, dragging it to the trash and then removing it from his drive. Gone. Done.

There was a knock on the office door. The door opened, and Gabriel Garcia, a thick-set lawyer with an equally thick black moustache, entered Lazaro's spacious office, followed by a young paralegal and Lazaro's executive secretary.

Lazaro's secretary shut the door gently behind her, her expression composed and yet there was sadness in her eyes.

"We're ready," Señor Garcia said, opening his briefcase. Lazaro nodded and they all wordlessly moved to the conference-style table in the corner. Each took a chair, the mood tangibly oppressive, deafeningly silent.

Lazaro's secretary, dressed today in an unusually severe black suit with a cream silk blouse, placed stacks of binder-clipped papers on the table. Lazaro wanted to say something to Imelda, reassure her somehow, but the words stuck in his throat.

As Imelda passed out the paperwork and the paralegal passed out pens, Lazaro felt Gabriel's gaze, the lawyer's expression brooding.

Lazaro was grateful Gabriel didn't attempt conversation. Lazaro couldn't handle conversation. He could barely go through the motions right now.

Zoe glanced at her watch for the umpteenth time in the past hour. Where was Lazaro? He was supposed to be here ages ago. Daisy had delayed dinner twice now. What was holding him up?

Zoe glanced at her watch yet again. Dante had gone to phone the office and Zoe glanced at Daisy where she sat on the couch with the baby. Daisy looked tired. It was growing very late, even for a fashionable Argentine dinner.

Chewing on the inside of her cheek, she tried to hide her growing anxiety. Something urgent must have come up at the office for him to be delayed so long. She didn't want to think what urgent could mean.

The door to the living room opened and Dante appeared with a stranger, a dark-suited stranger with thick black hair and a thick black moustache.

"Zoe," Dante said quietly. "Come with me."

Something was wrong, terribly wrong. Zoe's nerves screamed on edge. She glanced at Daisy then Dante. "What's happened?"

"We'll talk in the library."

She shot Daisy another glance. Daisy looked as baffled as she did. "No, let's stay here. I want Daisy here."

Dante and Gabriel Garcia stepped into the living room and Dante closed the doors. Zoe watched as the man with the black moustache opened his briefcase and pulled out a sheath of papers and a pair of reading glasses. He slipped the glasses onto the bridge of his nose.

"I am Gabriel Garcia. I am your husband's attorney."

Her stomach cramped hard. She slid into a chair. "Why isn't he here? Where is he?"

Dante gazed at her steadily. "He's not coming tonight."

"Why not?"

"He's going away, Zoe, and he's asked Señor Garcia to handle the paperwork for him."

"The paperwork? Paperwork for what? I don't understand—"

"Lazaro has given everything away."

"Given what away?" She'd begun to shake, hands, arms, legs.

"Everything. His corporation, his shares of stock, his hotels. Everything. He's given it back to the Galván family, to be divided between the baby and me."

Her eyes hurt. She blinked, as if she could get the gritty feeling out. "And Lazaro?"

"He leaves Argentina tonight."

CHAPTER TWELVE

THANK God, Lazaro's attorney knew where Lazaro was going, and knew the time Lazaro was leaving. Señor Garcia hadn't wanted to break Lazaro's confidence but Dante wouldn't let Gabriel leave the house without telling them what Lazaro intended.

Dante immediately called for his driver and instructed the chauffeur to drive Zoe to the harbor as quickly as possible. Lazaro was scheduled to leave by boat, chartering a friend's one-hundred-and-twenty-foot yacht for an extended trip along the South American coast. Dante knew the yacht Lazaro would be sailing and described its location to Zoe.

It was dark when she reached the dock. Lights glowed from the tethered yachts, strands of white lights strung from some ship masts, music coming from others.

She found the massive yacht exactly where Dante said it would be anchored. The boat swayed on the water. The engine already hummed. Yellow light shone from within.

Zoe hesitated and then before she could take a step, she heard Lazaro's voice from the deck. He was speaking Spanish, sounded as though he were giving instructions. She was just about to shout his name when he jumped down a ladder and appeared before her.

"*¡Dios!* Zoe!"

She backed up a step, felt a tremor of anguish. He was really going to leave. He was going to pull anchor and sail away, leave her behind, just like that. "Where are you going?"

He didn't say anything. He shook his head.

The activity continued on the yacht's upper deck. She heard the sound of boxes being stacked and a scrape of metal.

She stared past him to the yacht, where moonlight glinted off the glossy white finish. Her heart seemed to fill her throat. He hadn't even planned on saying goodbye. He was just going to go. Just going to get on that damn white yacht and leave her behind.

"I don't understand." Her voice came out strangled. Good Lord, she was close to tears. Not just a couple tears, but horrible wrenching sobs.

How could he do this?

How could he do this *to her?*

Fury overrode her shock. "Am I that easy to let go?" she choked, heat surging through her.

"Zoe—"

"Am I just someone you throw away?"

"It's for you I do this."

"*Bull.*" She jerked straight, shoulders squared, nails digging into her clenched fists.

She stared him up and down. He wore jeans and white canvas deck shoes. Sailing shoes. He really had intended to go.

"What about me?" she demanded huskily, fighting to keep the pain contained, fighting to keep some vestige of control.

His face was expressionless. "You don't need me."

"But I want you."

"You'll get over me."

She was shivering on the inside, shivering with alternating waves of hot and cold, rage and grief. "And not saying goodbye would help?"

His brow furrowed. "You're young, Zoe. You can have anything you want in life—"

"Fine. I want you."

"No."

"You said I could have anything I want, well, I want you." Although right now she didn't know why. He was awful, hateful, cruel. He was going to leave her. Leave her. Just like her father, and her mother, and Daisy… "Damn you, Lazaro."

His shoulders lifted, a careless Latin shrug. "It's better this way. I'm not the right man for you."

"Too bad. Too late. I love you." And she did, even if she was furious. Even if she was scared out of her mind. All she knew was that she couldn't, wouldn't, let him go without a fight.

"Zoe, I've given it away. I'm not destitute, but I'm not the man with twenty million in the bank, either."

She trembled with anger. "When did I ever want you for your money? When did I ever need you for *things?*"

"Money is important."

"Money pays the bills, but money doesn't buy happiness. Trust me on this one."

"My mother died because she didn't have enough money."

"Your mother died because she didn't have enough love." Zoe's anger deflated and her heart suddenly felt tender. She saw him as he must have been as a child. He would have been gentle. He would have adored his mother, and he would have desperately wanted to protect her. "But, Lazaro, I'm not your mom, and I'm not Daisy. I'm Zoe. I'm a simple person and I have simple needs. I need you. That's all."

"Easy to say now—"

"No, it's not easy to say now. I'm stunned at everything that's happened, and hurt that you'd actually leave me without saying goodbye, that you'd send a lawyer to deliver the news."

"I didn't mean it that way. I only wanted to make it easier."

"Easier? For whom? If you go now, my life will never be the same. Part of me will shrivel up and die."

"Zoe—"

"It's true," she continued urgently. "I feel alive when I'm with you, I feel like me when I'm with you, I feel like the Zoe I was always meant to be."

"But I want to protect you. I need to protect you."

"From who, Lazaro, from what?"

He didn't answer and she suddenly understood. He was trying to protect her from himself. She moved forward, moved to touch him, but he took an unsteady step back.

"You're not protecting me if you break my heart," she added softly. "You're not helping me at all."

"I want you to be happy, Zoe."

"And I am, with you, happier than I've ever been,

happier than I've ever dreamed. Like you, I've lost people I've loved, and felt great pain, and yet when I'm with you I only feel hope. I only see possibility." She reached out to him again and this time he didn't move away. She placed a hand against his chest, just above his heart. "Don't take the hope away. Please, *corazón*."

He closed his eyes, passed a hand over his face. "Zoe, I can't stay here. I can't live here anymore."

She understood. Too well. The memories here would always be hard, the past would always be with them, the failures as well as the mistakes. "Then we go somewhere else. We start a new life in a new place."

He didn't answer and yet she felt his heart thudding beneath her palm. Leaning forward, Zoe kissed his chest, kissed the place where she felt his heart. "Just take me with you. Keep me with you."

"I want to." His voice broke, the words almost strangled in his throat. "God knows I want to."

"Then do it."

He stood very still. He opened his eyes and stared at a point beyond her shoulder, a place on the water where the moon reflected high and white and full. A small yacht motored out and the inky water churned white and foamy in the wake.

Slowly he shook his head. He looked defeated. "I don't want to be cold anymore."

"You aren't that man, Lazaro. You haven't been that man for a long, long time."

"I need to start fresh somewhere else."

"Yes."

"But I don't know where to go. I've never belonged any place—'' He broke off, looked down at her, and reached out to touch her cheek. "I've never felt accepted until I found you."

She moved into his arms, felt him draw her close and she let out a quivery breath.

He held her even tighter. "Have you thought about Kentucky?"

Zoe squeezed her eyes shut as a wave of longing swept through her, the longing so intense that tears burned the back of her eyes. *Kentucky. Her father. The farm.*

But she held the emotion in, and fought for control.

"You wouldn't want to go home?" he persisted gently.

Zoe gazed up into his face. "You'd go to Kentucky for me?"

"I'd go to the moon if that's what you wanted."

"I don't want to go to the moon."

"Then how about Kentucky?

"You'd really do that for me?"

"Of course. I'd do anything for you." Moonlight drenched his profile, easing the hard grim lines of his face, gentling the length of his nose and the curve of his mouth. He traced the shape of her lips with the tip of his finger. "I love you."

Her heart contracted, a sharp swift knotting that made her ache. "Then don't you dare leave me."

"I won't."

"And yes, I'd love to go home, back to Kentucky. I miss my dad so much, but not if you don't want to."

"I want for you to be with your family again. I want us to be a family. I've never had a family…until I found you."

Her eyes burned and she blinked, unwilling to cry. He clasped her face, fingers spanning her jaw, and gazed into her eyes for the longest time, saying nothing and yet she knew what he was thinking, knew what he was feeling. They'd always had this bond, always had a special connection.

Lazaro's voice sounded rough. "I don't know that I'd make a very good horse breeder, but I'd try."

"You don't have to breed horses, you could do business, start a new business—"

"It'd be difficult."

"Which you should like. You love challenges. You're thrilled by that which is impossible."

He suddenly laughed, his voice warm and husky in the night, and with the water sloshing behind them and the boats creaking at the dock, the world felt full of beauty, and opportunity. "You know me too well."

She grimaced ruefully. "And I still love you."

The laughter faded from his eyes. "I am the luckiest man alive."

"We're both lucky."

He caressed her cheek. "I wish I hadn't put you through so much—"

"Things happen. Life happens."

He kissed her, his lips covering hers, drinking her breath, drawing her into him. A shiver of pleasure raced beneath her skin and her body warmed, wanting him, needing him, craving him, but she couldn't forget that he'd nearly left without her, that if she hadn't rushed to the wharf he might have gone.

Zoe's fingers curled into a fist and she pounded once on his chest. "How could you even think about going without me? How could you do that?"

A tugboat horn sounded in the distance, a low distinct cry that echoed off the tethered boats and slap of waves against the wooden pier.

"I don't know," he answered at length. "I just wanted what was best for you."

Gritty tears filled her eyes. "You're what's best for me."

He reached up to wipe the tears from her lower lashes. "I don't deserve you, Zoe, but if you're willing to give me another chance, if you're willing to try to make this work, I will be yours, and only yours, for the rest of my life."

"Yes."

He continued to wipe the tears from beneath her eyes, his touch infinitely gentle, and loving. "I'm glad my mother never knew the harsh things I've said and done, but I do wish she could have known you. I wish she would have seen what a beautiful woman I married, and I'm not talking about the outside, Zoe, I'm talking about your heart."

A sob formed inside of her. She was about to lose the last of her self-control and he brought her against him, wrapped his arms around her.

"I love you," she whispered, remembering their vows, remembering the commitment she'd made to him, a commitment she fully intended to keep. "For richer or poorer, in sickness or in health—"

''Till death do us part.''

''Amen.''

He laughed softly, and it was the sweetest, warmest sound she'd ever heard. The darkness that once haunted his eyes was gone, and only light remained— the whitewash of moonlight, the warmth of his heart, the flicker of hope.

''Over time, after we settle into life in Lexington, maybe I can build my business again,'' he said. ''I did it once, I don't see why I can't do it again.''

''You can do anything you set your mind to.''

He blinked, a sheen in his silver-gray eyes, tenderness in the curve of his lips. ''Life's good, isn't it?''

Smiling through her tears, she nodded and drew his head back down to hers. ''Life's great.''

Modern Romance™
...seduction and
passion guaranteed

Tender Romance™
...love affairs that
last a lifetime

Sensual Romance™
...sassy, sexy and
seductive

Blaze
...sultry days and
steamy nights

Medical Romance™
...medical drama on
the pulse

Historical Romance™
...rich, vivid and
passionate

MILLS & BOON

Winner at

2001 IDEA INTERNATIONAL
DESIGN
EFFECTIVENESS
AWARDS

MAT5

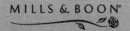

MILLS & BOON®

Modern Romance™

THE ARRANGED MARRIAGE by Emma Darcy

Set in the sugar-cane plantations of North Queensland, this is the steamy, sexy and emotional first book in Emma Darcy's incredible Kings Of Australia trilogy! Alex King is the eldest grandson of a prestigious family – and it's his duty to expand the King empire. He must also choose a bride and father a son…

THE DISOBEDIENT MISTRESS by Lynne Graham

Another winner from Lynne Graham, featuring her classic blend of romantic fantasy, spellbinding passion and a pinch of wry humour! The ruthless and sexy Sicilian tycoon Leone Andracchi needs Misty to pose as his mistress for a couple of months! In return he'll help her out of her financial difficulty. How hard can it be…?

THE GREEK TYCOON'S REVENGE by Jacqueline Baird

Powerfully written, very intense and extremely passionate with another of Jacqueline's trademark alpha male heroes! On holiday in Greece, Eloise had fallen in love with Marcus Kouvaris. But he suspects her of defrauding his uncle. Can Eloise persuade Marcus that she's innocent – and claim his love?

THE MARRIAGE PROPOSITION by Sara Craven

With a unique twist on a popular theme, and fresh, lively writing, this is a really gripping read! Paige can hardly believe she is married to Nick Destry. He's confident, sexy – and ruthless. But does he love her? He will have to prove it!

On sale 7th June 2002

Available at most branches of WH Smith, Tesco, Martins, Borders, Eason, Sainsbury's and most good paperback bookshops.

0502/01a

Coming in July

❦

The Ultimate
Betty Neels
Collection

❦

* A stunning 12 book collection beautifully packaged for you to collect each month from bestselling author Betty Neels.

* Loved by millions of women around the world, this collection of heartwarming stories will be a joy to treasure forever.

Available at most branches of WH Smith, Tesco, Martins, Borders, Eason, Sainsbury's and most good paperback bookshops.

2 Books
and a surprise gift!

We would like to take this opportunity to thank you for reading this Mills & Boon® book by offering you the chance to take TWO more specially selected titles from the Modern Romance™ series absolutely FREE! We're also making this offer to introduce you to the benefits of the Reader Service™ —

- ★ FREE home delivery
- ★ FREE gifts and competitions
- ★ FREE monthly Newsletter
- ★ Books available before they're in the shops
- ★ Exclusive Reader Service discount

Accepting these FREE books and gift places you under no obligation to buy; you may cancel at any time, even after receiving your free shipment. Simply complete your details below and return the entire page to the address below. *You don't even need a stamp!*

YES! Please send me 2 free Modern Romance books and a surprise gift. I understand that unless you hear from me, I will receive 4 superb new titles every month for just £2.55 each, postage and packing free. I am under no obligation to purchase any books and may cancel my subscription at any time. The free books and gift will be mine to keep in any case.

P2ZEB

Ms/Mrs/Miss/Mr ....Initials ....

BLOCK CAPITALS PLEASE

Surname...

Address...

....

....Postcode ....

Send this whole page to:
UK: The Reader Service, FREEPOST CN81, Croydon, CR9 3WZ
EIRE: The Reader Service, PO Box 4546, Kilcock, County Kildare (stamp required)

Offer not valid to current Reader Service subscribers to this series. We reserve the right to refuse an application and applicants must be aged 18 years or over. Only one application per household. Terms and prices subject to change without notice. Offer expires 30th August 2002. As a result of this application, you may receive offers from other carefully selected companies. If you would prefer not to share in this opportunity please write to The Data Manager at the address above.

Mills & Boon® is a registered trademark owned by Harlequin Mills & Boon Limited.
Modern Romance ™ is being used as a trademark.